# Vengeance in Disguise

Ian MacMillan

Published by New Generation Publishing in 2021



First Edition



Paperback ISBN: 978-1-80031-460-3
Ebook ISBN: 978-1-80031-459-7

**www.newgeneration-publishing.com**

New Generation Publishing

*I would like to dedicate this book to Luggy, an old friend in both meanings of the word 'old'. He has helped me both with ideas and detailed comments on my writing. I shall not say his real name as I think he is the only one who knows what it is. His nickname however came from the 72nd Boy Scouts for his cooking skills at summer camp near Dunbar. He invented a fantastic sweet for us to enjoy; it was a sliced Swiss roll dipped in setting fruit jelly. Luggy is shorthand for Luigi, back then one of Glasgow's famous tally chefs.*

## Contents

# Chapter 1

## Ardnamurchan

David Mackay sat quietly. His back was firmly pressed into the rocky headland which looks out over Kilmory Bay. He had always loved this place and regarded it as one of Ardnamurchan's most beautiful locations. A spot ideal for resting, to contemplate the world. The sea in front of him was full of islands with jagged peaks mainly Jura, Muck and Rum. A great location beyond which, if only you could see for a few thousand miles, he would have been looking at the coast of America.

Just a few months ago, his family had seemed secure, settled and very comfortable. As Chief Executive of a company in Inverness providing renewable energy his position seemed stable for as long as he wished providing health did not intrude. His income easily covered the expenses of the pleasant middle-class life his family enjoyed. They lived in a large, detached, stone house in Poolewe, a village just north of Gairloch in Wester Ross. David's wife, Helen, to whom he had been married for twenty-three years, had recently been appointed head of the local primary school and enjoyed her work thoroughly.

He and his family had always loved their holidays in this very attractive part of Scotland's West Highlands. David looked out to where the islands were clearly delineated against the setting sun. Even though he was a distance away he could hear the soft, rhythmic swish of the tide intermingled with the occasional plaintive cry from the sandpipers.

But this time, David's thoughts were far, far away. He kept shaking his head as he desperately tried to face up to the enormity of the devastating change which had overtaken his life.

Just a few months ago his family seemed so settled. You

would have thought that nothing could take that away from them. He and Helen had three children. They had thought their family was complete with the first two, a girl they named Margaret and a boy, Ross. Then along came a completely unexpected, nor planned arrival, Eilidh. Their oldest, Margaret, graduated with a good degree in commercial accountancy from Glasgow University. She was now living in a rented flat in Glasgow, enjoying both her new job and new husband, Angus. The two were also looking forward very much to the birth of their first baby, as were the delighted grandparents to be.

Ross, their second child, had always loved nature. Many was the time David had spent with him netting sea creatures from the rocky pools on the beach below. So it was no surprise to them that Ross had chosen to study environmental science, he also got a good degree, from Aberdeen University and was now working from that city assessing oil companies' work and how they affected the environment from their drilling rigs in the North Sea.

Then, please don't tell any of them this, but just when they had assumed that their family was complete with a girl and a boy, along came Eilidh; to be honest, his special one of all of them. It was therefore no surprise that she was named after the love of David's life, her name is the Scottish Gaelic form of Helen.

The only one left at home had been Eilidh. Eilidh, the dark-haired, blue and twinkling- eyed daughter he loved so well had been showing signs of the beautiful woman she would become.

Eilidh, now twenty years old, had begun the second year of a degree course at Inverness University. She was taking a course in theatre management. David and Helen were over the moon at her success and at how much she was starting to look forward to a new career. But recently everything had changed. Over the last eighteen months she had been showing signs of turning into the rebellious teenager that everybody talks about. She was becoming sullen and uncommunicative, not taking care of her appearance, even withdrawing from her brother and sister. That was in the previous September. David was shattered as he recalled her meeting and falling headlong in love with an older man who seemed to have decided to become a lifelong student at the city's university.

Helen, in particular, was very careful not to let Eilidh know how they disapproved of her choice. They did not put any restrictions on her social life. Eilidh had dyed her lovely, dark hair to create a horrific mix of blonde and purple and took to wearing what looked like kids' clothing from back in the sixties. David and Helen had lengthy discussions about what they could do as parents to help their daughter pick up a constructive way of life again. But they, together with strong advice from relatives and friends, decided that this was hopefully just an extreme reaction to the hormonal surge youngsters had to work their way through. That it would pass and all they could do in the meantime was to be there for her always, being totally supportive.

# Chapter 2

# Tragedy

Then out of the blue his life and hopes for his youngest daughter changed out of all recognition. Eilidh, aged twenty, was in the second year of her degree. She had always enjoyed acting and had loved being part of her school's dramatic society. So her decision to take a degree in theatre management was no surprise to her family.

David and Helen had been worried by tales of the bohemian lifestyle some of the students adopted and, while she was sharing living in her rented student accommodation with them, Eilidh was always involved with whatever her mates got up to. Their concerns had increased in recent years as the drug dealers were increasingly using what were called 'county lines' where youngsters would be recruited to sell drugs even in very remote country areas. Even where they lived, in the little village of Poolewe, they would hear and read about very sad stories of vulnerable young people becoming addicted.

Therefore, to make their daughter's life safer, David and Helen purchased a small flat for her in a nice area in the Highland's capital city. Eilidh had, for the first year of her studies, seemed to be living the perfect student life. She was popular and thoroughly enjoying her course. She had a nice group of friends, liked living in Inverness and still kept in regular contact with her family by phone, email and texts. Eilidh also visibly seemed to love coming home in the holidays.

Then at the start of her second year, everything changed. Helen was contacted by one of Eilidh's lecturers. She wanted to let them know of her concern that Eilidh was hardly ever attending her classes whereas the previous year she had hardly missed any. David phoned Eilidh and said that he wanted to come and see her, to stay over, have a meal out and talk about how things were going. Eilidh was not at all keen so he gave her no option but to agree. When she opened the flat door, David was horrified. She lived in a mess, was wearing hippie clothing, her hair was shaggy and uncared for. She and her flat were just a tip. What the hell had happened to their neat, well brought up daughter? There was also an acrid, sweet smell hanging in the air. From reading his thriller and spy books, David suspected it was cannabis or some other drug.

When David confronted Eilidh she flew into a vicious temper, accused him of not loving or caring for her, then, at the height of her tantrums, he heard a key being turned in the lock. The door opened and in came a young man. Eilidh quietened down and introduced him to David as Brodie, saying that he was a fellow student living with her just now. Eilidh insisted that he join them for a meal at the Rajah, Inverness's oldest Indian restaurant.

Over the meal, well lubricated with lager, David probed and soon actively disliked Brodie. He came from a wealthy family, was obviously spoilt and David judged him to be very much the wrong man for their daughter.

Back home the next day Helen was horrified to hear his news but what to do? Many of their friends and neighbours had encountered problems as their children entered the late teenage years. The most common advice was to stay away, let them go through this phase but always ensure that they know you're always there for them. And so they restrained themselves into not acting, albeit very fearful that this was just the wrong approach.

About four months later came the phone call from hell. 'Good morning, Mr. Mackay. Detective Sergeant Mackenzie here, from Inverness police station. I am afraid I have some very bad news for you. Early this morning, officers called at the flat your daughter Eilidh occupied. One of her friends, who wishes to remain anonymous, said he was very concerned that he could not get in contact with her, that she might be ill. When we called and could not gain entry we forced the door and found Eilidh lying on the floor. The doctor who was called pronounced her dead and, I hate to have to tell you this, it is believed that drugs were involved.'

'Oh my God, where is she?'

'She is currently on her way to the mortuary.'

'Can I see her?'

'Yes of course, but you might have to wait a bit while the people there have had time to properly attend to her.'

David, for the rest of his life, would never forget the sight that awaited him and Helen. When they stepped into the mortuary, the medical technician led them to a metal table and gently removed a white sheet from Eilidh's head. She looked so beautiful. Her hair had been tidied. Her face was worn thin, and drawn, but the beautiful young girl just lay there as if she was in a deep sleep.

The next few days were a nightmare. They had to contact family and friends, sorting out all the arrangements. There were lots of forms to fill in and meetings with the funeral directors to organise the burial. It was over two weeks before they were able to proceed. The quiet, stone church in Poolewe was jam-packed with mourners. Some of these people they had not seen for many years. Many had travelled long distances to be with them in their sadness. A large group of Eilidh's fellow students were also there. Pam, the Episcopal minister, dressed in a white gown and bearing a gold cross, spoke kindly of their daughter's life. It was particularly emotional as Pam had known Eilidh since she was a little girl.

David suggested to Helen that he should take some time off work so that they could be together and try to recover from their awful loss. But she told him that work would do him good. Helen said that she would try her best to pick up her life again.

Then, three weeks later, David was called into a special board meeting. The Chairman told him that all the staff at the company were really sympathetic and deeply sorry to see David's suffering, so they had all clubbed in to establish a fund which the company would contribute to, so that David and his wife could have a really good holiday, somewhere far away in glorious sunshine; a chance to escape for a while from their grief.

In better days, Helen had suggested that the two of them should celebrate their silver wedding anniversary with just such a break in lovely weather. To find time to spend with one another and thought that Mauritius would be ideal. David's PA, Ann Davies, and Helen had become friends, in fact quite close friends. David realised that Helen must have told Ann of her hopes for such a happy occasion. It was Ann who had suggested the idea to the company.

David was delighted with this generous offer from his office and left work straight away to drive home fast to Poolewe to share the good news with Helen.

When David opened the front door, he called out his wife's name, 'Helen'. The lack of response and quiet made him uneasy. Shouting out her name again he charged up the stairs. Something led him directly to the spare bedroom. His world stopped. There she was, hanging from one of the roof beams. He could see how she had done it. Helen had taken his hammer and a roofing hook from his toolbox. She had secured it into the beam, tied a noose from their clothesline round her neck, climbed up on a chair which she then had kicked away. On the bed there was a letter lying waiting for him, a brief note saying how sorry she was, and how much she loved him. That she had tried, but just could not get over her daughter's death and needed to end her own life. The sickening pallor on her face told him all he needed to know; she had followed Eilidh, Helen was dead.

Somehow David got through Helen's desperately sad funeral hugely helped by Margaret and Ross. A week later David sat, mourning the loss of his wife and daughter in his back garden. Apart from his surviving daughter and son, what the hell was left, what was he going to do with the rest of his life? He decided he needed to go back to where it all had started, back to Ardnamurchan.

# Chapter 3

## Árdnamurchan again

His journey took him to Inverness then down by Loch Ness and the Caledonian Canal to Fort William. Just south of there, the Corran car ferry took him the short distance across Loch Linnhe to Ardgour in Sunart. He then travelled across Ardnamurchan to Acharacle where he had booked into the Loch Shiel Hotel which he knew from the old days. This was back before his family had been born. He and Helen as newlyweds had decided that, apart from their exotic honeymoon, they would visit parts of their own country which they did not know.

The next morning, having worked his way through a full Scottish breakfast, a feast of cholesterol, he drove to Kentra and the parking area he knew. He set off just carrying his back pack which contained the packed lunch the hotel had provided. He hiked over to the south side of the bay then turned off onto the forestry track which took him west, over a short peninsula to reach his destination, the gentle hillside above the stunningly beautiful beach known in English as the singing sands. It is said that, at a certain stage of the tide, the sand will sing to you as you walk along it. Its other claim to fame is that there is buried Viking treasure on or near it. Over the years, in spite of many family holidays, they had never found any, even though the kids loved searching and listening to the stories he made up about Viking warriors.

Now David sat back in the heather. He didn't notice the gentle honey-sweet smell of the blooming heather. He didn't notice the white breakers out to sea, nor how the waves were building up to a height of almost 4 feet before crashing on to the lovely, pale, golden, sandy beach below him. His eyes didn't even see the purple shadowed outlines of the islands in front of him. His eyes could not see, they were so blurred with tears.

Gradually his mind started to focus in on hatred of those who had been responsible for Eilidh's untimely death, and now his dearly loved wife Helen. His hatred of them grew. Those swine who made their ill-gotten gains by selling drugs to susceptible youngsters.

Now his hatred had grown to such an extent that it was the driving force forward for his life for the foreseeable future. David decided with crystal clarity that those who were responsible for this horrific trade would suffer and suffer terribly at his hands. He knew damn well that vengeance would not bring him complete peace of mind but angrily hoped it might save some other parent from going through the same hellish period.

He planned to allow a year of his time in which to create maximum disruption to those involved in this evil trade which seemed to be sweeping across the country damaging many youngsters. He had been particularly disgusted when he read in the newspaper about 'county lines', gangs recruiting very young children from outside their schools to act as local dealers. They usually selected youngsters from broken homes or with mental health issues. This was a very cunning although an extremely evil way of ensuring the criminals were safe from investigation.

Within the year, allowing a generous one month for each, David made up his mind to target five of the nation's head gangsters. Each of these gangsters plied their trade over one of Britain's main cities and the surrounding area. He would ensure that all information he gleaned from these swine, would be publicised first by the press then passed onto the police. He grimly relished the thought that some of the information might have to be extracted by torturing these thugs.

David used the UK road map he kept in his car and circled five locations which fitted his bill. From those he decided he needed a base in the area around Cambridge and another in the Scottish borders, also to have a further secluded hideaway where he could take breaks and work on his plans. However, he was totally determined to carry out his campaign without leaving any trace or even a hint of where he lived and who he was. Without doubt both gangsters and the police would try very hard to find him. He was not particularly concerned for his own safety but no harm or even a threat of it should ever come anywhere near Margaret and Ross. With this in mind he next searched for a central location from where he could do his homework. He decided on the area around Derby and found a large, deserted farmhouse in an isolated area which he rented for a year. It was only fifteen minutes' drive from the town. Now it was time to get down to work.

# Chapter 4

## Inverness, planning

**Campaign** David's overall plan was to identify some of the leading figures in this horrible drugs trade, disable them temporarily and transport them to a suitable building. He would keep them secured for up to two weeks in very uncomfortable surroundings using drugs and torture as necessary to make them talk. Telling them in no uncertain terms that their time as a leader of the dealers who created this profitable but criminal business was at an end. That, if he learnt that they had returned to their old ways by again becoming involved in dealing in drugs, he would kill them. Failure to comply would result in their death.

David would then demand two more things from them. First a full account which he would record of their life as a drugs baron. Who they employed, where they obtained the drugs etc. Also did they have any information about similar leading figures elsewhere in the country? Second, that after he released them, they would each pay £200,000 into a bank account that he had opened to fund his campaign.

This required David selecting a number of targets in major cities across the country and also finding accommodation like a disused remote building which could be rented for use as their prison. He would have a number of disguises, fake ID and obtain transport, weapons and equipment.

David caught the Westerbus from his home and booked into a central modest hotel for the night.

**Fake ID** That evening, late on, David walked up to each of the people on the main and side streets getting settled in to sleep out rough for the night. He asked each of them if they had an up-to-date driving licence. Eventually one man, a stick-thin, bearded type who spoke intelligently, told him that he did. That he'd become just too fond of the drink and lost his job and marriage. He told David that his name was Alan Carter. Now, he had fallen on hard times as social security payments had not come through and that was why he was in this desperate state.

David empathised with the man and said he would like to help. He asked Alan if he could borrow his driving license for a week. That he would pay him £200 for the privilege and a further £300 when he returned it. David explained that he had to create a false identity for a role he needed to fulfil. Alan had no problem at all agreeing, so then handed over the licence as David handed him the money.

**Finance** David returned to his home in Poolewe. The next morning he phoned a friend, Angus McGovern. He was branch manager for the bank in Gairloch. David asked him how much money he could raise using as security the £500,000 property and land that he owned. Angus straight away said up to £300,000. He said if necessary, the property would have to be valued but it was certainly worth that amount.

David arranged to meet him for a pint in the Old Inn. After catching up on their news they were onto their second pint when David said, 'Angus, there is something I want to discuss with you but it must remain confidential between us as it's about my family. Is that OK?'

'Of course, David, I am well known for my ability to keep secrets.'

David gave him a brief account of the hellish time he had been going through. Then gave him a rough outline of the campaign of vengeance he planned. He ended by explaining that that was the reason he enquired about raising funds but now he knew he could raise more than sufficient for his needs, he needed to find a way to access them without anyone's knowledge.

David said that he was going to adopt a fake identity and open up a bank account in that name, using a genuine driver's licence he had acquired. Into it he would transfer the funds he intended to raise and use them for the expense of his campaign. Also, that he would force the criminals he captured to pay money as some form of redress into the same account which he would then close and transfer the monies back to his personal account. David asked Angus if there was any way he could do all of that without any risk of his personal details being discovered.

Angus sat quietly as David bought them another round.

'David, there is no way legally that I can help you achieve your objectives. However, we have known one another a long time and I am horrified to hear your very sad story. I well understand why you want to have a go at these swine and wish you all the best. The only thing that can be done is that I will personally open up the account you wish and oversee all transfers, without the knowledge of my bank or our accountants.'

David sat for a while, speechless. He had hoped Angus would help him but never expected such a tremendous outcome. He thanked Angus deeply then said 'I know you would be risking a lot so I will make sure that you are appropriately rewarded.' Angus tried to brush this aside as his offer was on the basis of friendship, but David said that he knew that Angus was risking his career and pension for him so would insist, Angus accepted the remuneration, and asked to be given two weeks to set it all up.

A fortnight later, David transferred £300,000 to the new bank account in the name of Alan Carter, then returned to his hotel in Inverness.

**Guns** The next evening he went to one of the nightclubs at the west end of the town. This one was a very popular venue for young people. There were two bouncers outside. David went up to the ugliest and most brutal-looking of them and asked if he could have a word in private. He said there was money involved. The man glowered at him but stepped aside. 'What do you want, you look a bit old for our young girls, fellow? Are you one of them kiddie snatchers?'

David said, 'No, it's nothing like that. I have no interest

in your club, its help I want from you. My young daughter is being threatened by a nasty, local thug, he's trying to get her to buy his drugs. I need to scare the shit out of him. As you can see, I am getting on a bit and have nothing like the body you have, otherwise I would have gone for him already. I need to buy a gun, can you help me find one?'

He said 'It'll cost you, mate.'

David explained that he was prepared to pay and pay handsomely. 'How's about I pay you £100 now and the same after I get the gun?'

'No fucking way, mate, £300 now or just bugger off.'

After David had paid up, the bouncer, who said his name was Sid, said 'Right, the guy you want is a Polish man called Jakob. He lives in Merkinch, do you know where that is?'

'No but I'll find it OK.'

'Here's his address. Tell him Sid sent you.'

The next afternoon David went to the property. It was a run-down council flat in one of the similar blocks which lined the street.

Jakob turned out to be a slim, pale man in tattered jeans. He asked how he could help. David explained that Sid had said he could supply him with guns. 'Yes, that's right, I can get you almost anything if you're prepared to pay up and it has to be cash. What is it that you are looking for?'

'I want a lightweight revolver fitted with a silencer. Also, two working hand grenades. Over and above that I need to get two stun guns each capable of knocking a big man flat.

'Wow mate, you are into some very heavy shit. This will really cost you!'

'That's OK, I have the funds.'

'Right, I can do all of that. It will take me a few days. I will charge you £700 for the gun and four boxes of ammo. The grenades will be £100 each. About the stun guns, you are talking about the very best, the most powerful on the market. I reckon I can knock the seller down to 200 per gun. So that makes a total of £1,300. You will pay me £1,000 now and the rest on collection.'

Jakob was completely taken by surprise when David just paid up, without any haggling, and left.

**Phones** David went into a phone shop he'd used before in the High Street. He explained that he was looking for three mobile phones and prepared to pay well for them. That he wanted them all altered so that each was untraceable and if possible, to have an app installed which would allow his voice to be disguised. The young boffin looked very wary of these two requests but changed his mind when David passed two £50 notes to him with a wink.

'Certainly sir, I can arrange for the voice to be faked but not to make the number untraceable. You are better just buying a number of phones and throw them away when you are finished with them. Just give me until the end of the week and they will be ready.'

**Targets** David decided on five target areas: London, Birmingham, Newcastle, Glasgow and Edinburgh. He knew Glasgow and Newcastle areas – from working there in in the early days of his career. He had some knowledge of Birmingham and Edinburgh from family occasions. Rather than start with Glasgow, he decided to avoid pointing the finger at his Scottish roots and therefore would start with London, the area he was most unfamiliar with. His attacks would obviously be dependent on how much, if any, news about his other attacks got out into the criminal underground. If anyone learned of his methods, they would be able to change their way of life and perhaps avoid a similar fate. Also, they would stand a fair chance of working out how he was likely to act on their own patch and arrange a suitable, extremely painful end to his life.

Now he puzzled over how to find out who was known to be the leading figure in the illegal drugs trade in each area. He decided to start at the foot of the drugs ladder and threaten a local dealer with pain unless they told all they knew about the character involved. He thought, depending on the success of that, he should next be making contact with one of the leading crime reporters at one of the most popular, national, daily newspapers.

**Transport** His plan was to use the drugs he would obtain, to knock out his victim without being seen unless in disguise. Then, after the man's bodyguards would inevitably call for an ambulance, he would arrive in uniform in an ambulance that he would have purchased and take the gangster to his hideaway. So over and above the ambulance he would need a wheelchair, ties to secure his captive, a driver's uniform and an alternative form of transport. There was no way he would use his own car as it could lead back to him but he thought buying a motorbike would allow him to get around.

David thought it unlikely that he could hope to take all five targets down without news of his captures leaking out to the gangs. It was likely that the ambulance, which of course was very distinctive, would be identified at some stage. Therefore, one more means of transporting his victims was needed. After a bit of thought he decided on a sizeable builder's van. He could dress up as a workman. That then required each of his hideaways to have a large garage where he could store the ambulance and van, so he needed garaging at Derby.

**Disguises** One advantage he had was the huge amount of reading he had enjoyed of crime and terrorism thriller books. Many of the ideas on how to go about his plan came from them or from movies, like 'Liam Neeson's *Taken*. He decided on three disguises. On each of them he would use contact lenses rather than his everyday specs. Then he would arrange to wear shoes with 2 inches added to the soles and heels to alter his height. He planned that his main outfit would have him seen as red-haired with a moustache and beard of the same colour. This man would be of slim build, helped by wearing a very tight woman's corset. He would be casually dressed in jeans and sweaters, unless when posing as an ambulance driver when he would don the relevant uniform.

The second disguise would be as a sewerage workman, overweight by using an inflatable cushion, and wearing worn boots, dirty overalls and a shabby cap. The last disguise would be as a prosperous, overweight business man wearing a smart suit, with glossy hair and a little, stylish moustache.

**Drugs** David needed a powerful knock out drug, capable of rendering unconscious his victims and their bodyguards. He decided to make contact with his niece Aileen, a qualified pharmacist, to seek her advice on what drugs to use which would disable someone by rendering them out for the count for about two hours.

**Base** David decided that he would seek a property for himself in the centre of the country, possibly in the vicinity of Derby with a garage where he, acting as a writer could also keep the disguises and all the equipment between his individual attacks. He would assume the role of a writer to explain the regular absences to any neighbours who became nosy in that he was away abroad on research. Thus, all of the campaigns could be completely separate from his own life and home in the Scottish Highlands.

**Height** David decided to spend the week in Inverness carrying out detailed research into the things and costumes he needed. He started by visiting Timpson's in the Newgate shopping centre. David went up to the counter, having waited until the shop was empty. The man said 'Yes, can I help you, sir?' He said 'I have a rather unusual request. I am wondering if be possible for you to add 2 inches to a pair of shoes. I am appearing in a pantomime and want to disguise my looks.' The man explained that due to the nature of the Timpson's organisation i.e. that they tend to employ only ex-criminals and set them on the right road, that such a trick would not be acceptable morally to them. It would be too much of a risk. So David asked him whether it would be possible to purchase the heels, he could then do the job himself. The man said, 'Yes, no problem. I think that can be arranged.'

**Spececs** His next visit was to Specsavers, again in the High Street. David asked about contact lenses, assuming this would require a visit to the optician. The young man said, 'No, we already have the specification from your last eye test. What I would suggest, is that you purchase a month's worth of disposable eye lenses, you put them in place daily. That would only cost you £11 a month. Then you could see how you get on and if everything's OK you could then buy more.' David was surprised that that it could be done so cheaply and agreed to collect them the following week.

# Chapter 5

## Derby, preparation

David travelled from his home in Poolewe down to Derby and the rented farmhouse. He took with him his laptop computer which he set up by a big wallchart on a desk with pens and memo pads and linked the computer to the Internet.

**Transport** Now that he had his main base, a new ID, and access to funds, his next priority was to be able to travel around anonymously. David decided to go back to the days of his youth and buy another motorbike. This would mean him being forgettable, dressed in leathers, a helmet, and goggles and the bike would be small enough to fit into the ambulance, and van.

He took the local bus into Derby and on to the main sales room. He test drove three bikes then settled on a second hand Triumph speed triple 1050, which was in excellent condition and handled like a dream. He acquired it for the asking price of £5,900.

It was now time to purchase an ambulance and associated equipment.

From internet searching he found that the main area for sales of used ambulances seemed to be an auction house in Merthyr Tydfil, in south Wales. David mounted his new bike and set off. It took him almost the full day to get there because, on the way he kept testing the bike by turning off and onto unmade roads, up steep hills and racing over rough forest footpaths. He booked into a B&B in Ebbw Vale, and went to the sales room the next morning. He did not take long to find the one he wanted and take it for a drive. It was a Mercedes Sprinter which had been run by a health authority, it handled very well. At the auction that afternoon, as soon as David offered the asking price of

£17,000, his fellow bidders backed off and let him have it. He thoroughly enjoyed his celebratory dinner, needless to say of Welsh lamb, in a very good pub that the sales boss had recommended. Then, because of his huge appreciation of choral music, he got a ticket for the local male voice choir. He had been very lucky to have landed on their evening of choral practice. Oh my God, how he enjoyed himself. Just sitting back, totally relaxed, and listening to delightful music. It was just what he was needing. The next morning, he set off. David was feeling quite chuffed with himself, things really seemed to be coming together well.

**Weapons** David knew almost nothing about the various types of guns, but from his many readings had concluded that he would need a stun gun and/or a Taser to temporarily disable his captives. The pistol he had already obtained from Jakob was only for his personal protection. He had absolutely no plan to injure or kill those gangsters who got in his way. He opened up his laptop and began research. He pondered how previous writers had gone about their work without the so easily accessible tools like Wikipedia. He was not bothered about people's comments criticising its accuracy, he was going to check everything out in detail.

First, he read up about the difference between a stun gun and a Taser. He learnt that stun guns, which could disable an opponent for a short time, just as he wanted, required the gun to be pressed into physical contact with flesh. The short burst of electric energy would flatten the victim. Whereas Tasers meant you having to fire an electric probe at your target from a distance up to 15 feet. Pressing the charger release would then completely disable the man. He learned to be very careful of cons, as this trade was not at all registered or licenced in the USA. Several claimed to have very powerful guns as measured by their voltage but this is not at all what one desires. The disabling was due to an electric shock i.e. current combined with time. The most accurate measurement was of the Microcoulombs emitted. Anything over 0.5 microcoulombs is sufficient to disable.

An attack of up to 5 seconds should be enough in most cases depending on the physique and fitness of the enemy.

It was clear that the best place to obtain both weapons was the USA where they are openly licensed for sale in several states.

He decided on a 'Sabre stun gun,' with a charge of 2.517 m*icrocoloumbs capacity,* that company's most powerful model, complete with batteries, a belt and holster could be obtained. The cost was around $30. David decided to obtain three of them. The gun weighed about 11/4 lbs so was no problem to carry in its holster.

He then thought that in case he needed to act at a distance possibly at several opponents so would also obtain 3 Tasers. The one which seemed to attract most favourable comments was a 'Pulse Taser' with a range of 15 feet. Two electric probes in thin wires were fired into the target, which would bring them crashing down to the ground. Its sales cost was $449. The gun had a battery warning indicator and came with a laser light for accurate aiming. Both weapons will penetrate anything but professional bodyguards' clothing.

So how to get hold of these. Well Jakob had come up with the goods so far without any problems. He telephoned his man in Inverness. Jakob said once again 'Yes, can do, but they will have to be smuggled over from the States. That'll cost you a pretty penny. With transport costs we are talking about £8,000 so if you send me £3,000, I will get things underway as fast as possible. Is that OK, and do you want me to courier the guns to you?'

'No, Jakob, I would like to see and test them with you. So I will call at your house.'

**Hideaways** David carefully examined the two areas he had selected near Cambridge. Using a marker pen he drew a circle around each of them on his RAC roadmap. One was just to the north, the other to the west of Cambridge. Both showed few towns and villages nearby and had only what seemed to be minor roads leading to them. He checked his satnav and found that from Birmingham it was roughly ninety miles, so about two to two and a half hours' travelling in the van. Then about sixty-two miles from London mainly using the M11, about one and a half hours' travel.

Aileen had said that the drug should last about 2 hours, so as long as he gave another jab half way all should be fine. Now David turned on his laptop and joined Google Earth adopting an alias. Using Street View he wandered all over the two areas, then marked a number of likely locations in remote areas. Next, he phoned the first of a number of local estate agents he'd obtained from a computer search.

His enquiry went as follows. 'Good morning, my name is Alan Carter. I am a writer seeking to rent a sizeable property in the following area. They must be very private and secluded. I need it to be isolated so that I have complete peace and quiet for my writing. I also need it to be sizeable as I will at times be bringing a group from my publishers to review my work. The property also has to have outbuildings capable of taking four vehicles, an abandoned farmhouse would be ideal. Can you help please?'

It took a whole day before David identified three potential targets. Again, he used his computer to stroll all round each area and the land adjacent to the buildings. He eventually chose one, a disused farmhouse not far from the village of Willingham which overlooked the Old West River. Now it was time to travel by motorbike down to Cambridge, meet the estate agent he had spoken to, and visit the building.

Three days later, David made his inspection, this was close to perfect. The farmhouse was on a gently sloping hillside, looking over a small stream. There were several outbuildings near to the big house. David entered into a six months leasehold of the farm which cost him £18,000. He put down a deposit of £5,000 and gave the agent details of the bank account he'd opened with Barclays in the name of Alan Carter. Next, he allowed himself a fortnight to have the necessary alterations made to the farmhouse. He contacted a local plumber who was taken completely by surprise, when David offered him a sizeable inducement to have a shower unit fitted within two weeks.

David next searched for a hideout in the southern Scottish Borders. This would mean that it would only be a two to three-hour journey time by van from his northern targets, Newcastle, Edinburgh and Glasgow. A large rural area to the west of Melrose seemed a likely spot. Using a combination of Google maps and his roadmaps, he drew up a boundary around the area similar to his approach down south.

Here he found an ideal property. This had been a handsome mansion house occupied by local aristocracy long ago. It was one of the many which had come to ruin over what must have seemed like ceaseless warring in the Borders. Then a nearby farmer had taken use of the land and some of the outlying structures. The main house was set in a commanding position looking down over the river called the Manor Water, it was situated on the eastern flank of Pikestone Hill.

**Costumes** After that David went into the central shopping arcade and down to where he had been told he would find a shop that sold costumes. He explained what he was looking for, to appear as a ginger-haired and bearded, moustached, skinny man dressed in casual clothing. Then the posh outfit and a chauffeur's clothing. 'No problem at all, sir, we can supply the wig and moustache, and will fit you out with the clothes you suggest. Just let me get your sizes noted. You should come to collect these at the end of the week.' David then went to an industrial warehouse and purchased a pair of green overalls, a pair of stout working men's boots, a safety helmet and workmen's gloves.

**Other equipment** He now had no option but to go shopping, something he hated, for the many small items that could prove vital to his campaign.

His list read - two boxes of ziplock ties, about 100 each; four syringes; a blood pressure monitor; an oxygen recorder for blood; and a red flashing light and siren. For all of these he would use his fake ID and claim to be working for a charity that looked after disabled people who at times needed to be taken to hospital sometimes urgently.

**Computer** He next went to Curries/Dixons. There he purchased a very powerful Lenovo laptop, a model 330 with a 15.6-inch screen and a laser printer, the best they had available. Also, David acquired a very powerful hard disc to act as backup for all the Information he gathered. He_had decided not to continue using his own computer in case it became tracked down. It was also very important to install good quality security at his hideouts. David took advice from a sales assistant and bought two camcorders with devices to allow recording in the dark. His foes were likely to attack in the night. They were also fitted with a motion sensor to enable remote activation and alarm. His total bill for all this equipment cost just over £3,000.

**Records** Now how best to store the treasure trove of information he was sure was just waiting for him. He bought five office briefcases complete with accordion file holders and two large boxes of blank CDs for the photos and recordings he would collect.

When he arrived back at his base, the duplicate driving license he had applied for in the name of Alan Carter was waiting there for him.

# Chapter 6

## Drugs

Now how to get hold of drugs? David's niece, Aileen, worked as the head pharmacist in Boots the chemist in Dundee. Aileen and he had always got on really well together. They liked one another and enjoyed having a laugh together. David phoned her at home.

'Oh, Uncle David, I'm so pleased to hear from you. How are you doing after that terrible time?'

'I am getting on a bit better Aileen, it seems that as time passes, I start to regain a little more and more of my old self, but I suppose I am, and always will be, still in mourning,' he said. 'Anyway, the reason I am phoning is that I am looking for a big favour from you using your technical expertise. I'm staying in a hotel by the A9. Can I take you out for a meal tomorrow night to your favourite restaurant of course?'

'Yes, certainly, David. I would be over the moon to see you and without any doubt you are welcome to anything in the world I can do to help.'

At 7 p.m. the next evening the two met and hugged one another fiercely. They had a lovely meal but when Aileen asked about what David wanted help with, he said 'Can we just wait till we have coffee and drinks and I'll tell you all about it?'

The pair found a quiet table in a corner where they would not be overheard. Their waitress brought coffee and drinks, then Aileen, burning with impatience, said 'Well, Uncle, what is it you want?'

'Aileen, it will not surprise you to hear that after what happened I have developed a real hatred for the scum who run the drugs trade which killed my daughter and her mother. I have decided to seek vengeance. I'm not going to tell you what I am planning to do but I can assure you that before this year is out, you'll be reading all about it in the news.'

'I understand completely, Uncle David, but please, don't put yourself at risk. We have all suffered enough loss and your son and daughter need you badly.'

'Don't worry Aileen, I will be extremely careful. I know the dangers of getting involved with these thugs and will use disguises and other means to ensure they have not the faintest idea who I am or where I come from. Now, as to what you can do to help. Without going into details, I want a sizeable quantity of clear liquid, a knockout drug. I would need enough for about fifty doses each strong enough to make a big man unconscious for between one and two hours.'

Aileen sat quietly nursing a drink. 'Yes, I can do that for you but it will take some time to produce and prepare that quantity of drugs, would a fortnight be OK?'

'No problem at all, Aileen.'

'Just be aware that these drugs will be very powerful. If any of your victims are in poor health that could be a risk to their life.'

'Aileen, that is the least of my concerns!'

They bade one another a fond farewell and arranged to meet in two weeks' time at the same restaurant.

Next David considered how to administer the drugs? For instance, in a bar without being seen? He contacted one of the major suppliers of children's toys who he had discovered was responsible for supplying the plastic eggs children would try to catch with a little crane in Fairground amusement machines. They would be filled either with sweeties, a ring or cheap earrings. They have two halves to be prised open. The company told him they arrive in boxes of a hundred. He ordered two to be sent to the property he was renting in Derbyshire.

When they arrived, he sat at the kitchen table practising his technique over and over again. Wearing a clear plastic surgical glove on his right hand he prised the egg in half, filled it with water, then put it back together again but not too firmly. He superglued the two halves onto the glove above his palm and closed the fist. Next, holding his hand over a glass, opened the fist fully, the halves parted and the liquid fell into the glass.

The next morning David woke feeling very pleased that things were going so well. He contacted his son and daughter and arranged to spend a few days with each of them, himself staying in a B&B rather than disturb their usual routine. The real reason for that was so that he could carry on with his mission. He planned to take the children out for meals, maybe to the theatre, and dine in their own homes with them. There he explained that unfortunately a big job off the coast of Norway, west of Stavanger, meant that he would be going away for maybe five to six months. Although he would have his mobile phone, reception would probably be poor or non-existent. However, David said that he would always be contactable on the net using his tablet. Both said that they would miss him, asked him to keep in regular touch, and wished him well.

So his plan looked like this. Two months allowed per victim, after each at least a week's break and rest at Derby. Therefore, an eleven month campaign, then some time somewhere nice, with what remained of his family

# Chapter 7

# London

David drove the ambulance from Derby down to Cambridge. The deserted farmhouse and outbuildings were ideally situated down a half mile drive from a minor road. There were no properties overlooking it. Also, a farm track ran through the woods at the rear onto another minor road. Just before the junction David wrapped the bike in its cover and hid it amongst the shrubbery ready, should he need to make an escape.

He then installed two security cameras, one by the entrance to the drive, the other by the front of the house. He connected them wirelessly to alarms in his new computer. Then he had a self-standing shower unit installed in the centre of the downstairs guest bedroom by a local plumbing firm. The tradesman couldn't understand what it was for until David explained it was to be used by his brother who had been severely disabled in a motorbike accident. David drilled four holes in its base and inserted rag bolts fixed securely into its floor, ready to chain the wheelchair very securely. A hosepipe was connected to the cold tap and looped across and into a position convenient for his prisoner to drink from.

For the prisoner's other needs David cut a circular hole in the seat of the chair. Things would be very smelly and messy. This would diminish and dehumanise his captive which fitted in very well with David's objectives. He then pinned old sheets across the windows so the room was completely dark. Then he positioned a strong light so that it would shine directly into the face of his victim. Now his cell was complete.

It was time to begin. Leaving the bike concealed and the building all ready to receive his 'guest,' David drove the two-hour journey he had calculated to the garage he had

rented in London, he had already, driven the builder's van there where it stood fuelled and ready for his escape, if necessary.
David had rented a substantial garage in an industrial area not far from the centre of London in case he had to use the van. It was easily large enough to take the ambulance and the van. He had a local garage make a flip down metal ramp for both the ambulance and van, hinged to fit over reels he installed at each rear door. He booked into a cheap hotel in Central London, dined well, then, with the help of three strong sleeping pills – thank you, Aileen – knocked himself out, into a deep sleep. Most of his early research into who was the head of the capital's criminal drugs scene would take place at night and he was determined to be alert and on his best form.

The next evening was a Friday. He spent the early hours walking all over the sleaziest part of Soho just getting to know the area. He went up to one of the bouncers standing outside a night club and, slipping the man a £20 note, asked where he could best find a street where he could meet both streetwalkers and drug dealers. In return for a further two £20s the man demanded, he learnt that his best bet was Curzon Lane.

Right enough, when he arrived there, he could see prostitutes leaning against almost every lamp post chatting to their mates until a car stopped beside them. He went up to the first one and told her he needed a fix then after that he might do some business with her. She grabbed the £20 note as if it were a lifebelt and told him that their main dealer was a man, a Jamaican called Abisai, who usually drove down the lane round about midnight selling to the girls.

At about twenty past twelve, David watched as a gleaming Porsche drove slowly down the lane stopping whenever one of the pros waved at him. He walked down to a quiet spot, then as the car approached him signalled it to stop.

'Yo man, you lookin'?' said the bejewelled, dark-skinned man with a Rastafarian hairstyle. He was dressed in a tight-fitting, silk, black suit with matching shirt and tie, added to which, believe it or not, he was sporting long, black earrings.

'I'm looking for quite a big supply of different drugs. I don't want to do business with you here, the prossies watch everything and the polis call regularly. Can you drive me to a quiet spot and we can have a chat?' Abisai was suspicious. The man was soberly dressed and spoke with a good quality voice, not at all like the punters he usually dealt with. But just as he was about to refuse, David half opened his coat to show a least five hidden pockets bulging with £20 notes.

'OK, get in Whitey,' Abisai said while turning the booming rap music back on. They drove about three blocks away into a deserted car park. Abisai was just reaching down for the sharp knife he carried as protection when he was slammed back into his seat as David bolted him three times with the stun gun.

When he came to and tried to sit up, he found that not only had each ankle been secured to its chair leg but David had twisted his arms round and fastened them with handcuffs behind his chair.

'What the fuck are you doing? Do you know who you're deali—'

He was slammed back into the chair again. When he came to it was to hear his torturer say, 'Right, Abisai, I do know what I am dealing with. You are a piece of shite lower than a water rat. Now, unless you tell me what I want, you are going to experience pain such as you've never had throughout your miserable life. Just nod if you understand. If you don't, I'll fire the gun until you do.' Abisai nodded, though was visibly furious.

'I want from you the names of the dealers you get your drugs from, including the most important one, you know, the big boss who supplies your evil trade.'

'Hey man, don't fire, I can't tell you that, if I become a traitor they will know straight away and there is nothing you can do to me worse than what they will do. My life will not be worth living.'

David just grabbed his left arm and twisted it round to the front. He placed an evil-looking pair of very sharp bolt croppers so that its claws enclosed the dealer's pinkie. A thin line of blood showed where they touched. 'Don't you do that you basta—' He jerked back, crying in pain and horror as he gazed, stunned, at the bleeding stump.

Without making any comment David moved the cutters to Abisai's ring finger. 'Anything to say yet, you piece of filth?'

Abisai shook his head, grimacing, then screamed in agony as the cutters snapped shut.

'Right, now you know I am not kidding. Unless you tell me what I want, I will snip off every finger, then slice open your slimy trousers and guess where I will put the cutters there, eh?'

Now, his spirit totally broken, Abisai told David all he knew including, most importantly, that the head honcho was a man called Mike, who had taken over the Krays' drugs empire.

Back in his hotel David very carefully read through all the information he could find on the Krays and the London drugs scene, articles from the press and information in Wikipedia. Unsurprisingly, the intelligence on London's head gangster was a great deal larger than on any other city.

Michael Gilmore, known as 'Mike' to one and all, was only one year old when his family left Falkirk for London. His father, Gregor, was a successful middleweight boxer. He had heard tales of big money to be earned in boxing in the capital city. Their council flat in Vallance Street in the east end of the city which they rented was not dissimilar to that they left behind in Scotland.

Gregor's uncle Barnie was involved with a boxing club and soon arranged fights for his cousin. This was in 1952 just as the to-be-famous, Kray twins were entering their twenty-year period of peak success.

Ronnie and Reggie had been competent boxers themselves, but their criminal records, plus being dishonourably discharged from the Army, meant they could no longer fight as professionals. Their love of the sport however had in no way diminished. They owned two boxing clubs and regularly attended matches all over London. The pair both liked the look of Gregor, whose excellent physique was attractive to them as a boxer but also to their sexual interests. But they really took to 'little Mike,' as he was called then. He used to come to watch his father, Gregor's, fights whenever possible. The wee lad was cheeky, sassy and had an infectious giggle.

It was not long before the twins were betting on Gregor as well as encouraging him to lose the odd contest on which they had gambled heavily. As the years advanced Gregor's health began to fail him and soon he had to give up the ring and worked giving tuition and training to young up-and-coming fighters. Also, the Krays began giving small jobs to Mike so he could earn a bit of pocket money and some sweeties. Later they allowed young Mike who now was a boxer himself to join their gang, The Firm. By this time, it was becoming widely recognised that the Krays were London's most powerful gangsters, and were often effectively in control of crime in London's east end.

Mike used to go round to see them at their home in Bethnal Green. The Krays' mother Violet, was a Cockney goddess. Her home was like a palace, always immaculate, and Mike's visits were always given a great welcome. Mike's life was going very well indeed, there was just one fly in the ointment

Ronnie was probably the first London gangster to come out openly as a homosexual, which was illegal in those days. Even though he had two marriages himself, throughout his life his sexual priority was men. Mike grew increasingly nervous when alone with him. It was the way Ronnie looked at him at times, as well as the occasional touch. He, like many others, also suspected that Reggie was also homosexual but decided to keep that to himself, as a secret.

In 1960 another gangster, Peter Rachman, gave the twins a nightclub in the west end. This was in lieu of payment for a big favour they had done for him. Being threatened with violence unless he paid large sums of protection money to one of their rival gangs. One of the twins' own men, a supposed hard man called 'Razor-face' had been turned by that gang and had been passing on information to them. Razor-face ended his life somewhat unhappily, being devoured by pigs on a farm rented by one of the Krays' henchmen.

In their new nightclub, one of the most popular in the city called Esmerelda's Barn, the twins were soon mingling with politicians and celebrities such as Diana Dors, Frank Sinatra, and Judy Garland. Also, they met with Cliff Richard, the Rolling Stones and the Beatles. Ronnie, boasting said, 'the Swinging Sixties were the best years of our lives, we were fucking untouchable.'

Then Mike got the lucky break which changed his life for ever. By now he was used to going into the various pubs the Krays used. He was sitting quietly in a corner having a sneaky fag, when he overheard some startling information. The Krays were planning their biggest coup to date. They intended to rob a security van delivering currency to the local banks. It appeared that the pair of thugs he was listening to were from another gang. They knew all about the robbery plan and meant to grab the proceeds for themselves.

They had found out that the Krays were to bring the loot back to a private room in a pub they owned and split it up amongst their followers. So the thugs would be waiting there with guns ready to grab the money, and if necessary shoot their way out.

Mike waited listening until the men left. Then he ran at full speed along the road to the club where he knew The twins were meeting their men. Mike yelled at the barman that he needed to see either Ronnie or Reggie, that it was bloody important. But the barman said 'Sorry, Mike, but they both made it very clear they were not to be disturbed.' Luckily just then, Reggie came out to see what the row was all about. When they heard what Mike had discovered the twins each gave him a huge hug saying, 'Well done, Mike, but now head off home, we have to plan what to do. We will see you later.' The burglary went off as planned but the two thugs, waiting in hiding in the back room, had a hellish surprise. The door burst open and six of The Firm crashed in, each pointing a pistol at them.

Meanwhile back home Gregor, Mike's father, was berating him for not telling him the news he'd overheard, when the doorbell went and in came Reggie and Ronnie. 'Gregor, your boy's done brilliantly. He's going to have a hell of a time with us. Which will be very much to your benefit as well. But now we have to deal with this.' They drove in their limo to a disused factory in an industrial estate. Reg opened the warehouse door and beckoned Mike in. The two thugs sat locked to pillars and looking terrified. They were both tied and gagged. 'Right, Mike, I want you to watch this, then you'll have a wee test.' He stepped up to the first of them, produced a gun and fitted it with a silencer then, without a pause, shot the man in the head.

'Well, what do you think of that?'

'It's all the bastard deserved, Reggie.'

'Could you do it?'

'Yes.' Nervously, as he had never held a gun before, Mike went up to the terrified other gangster, and shot him in the back of his head.

Ronnie then developed a deep intimate relationship with the Conservative politician Lord Boothby. This made the headlines in the Sunday Mirror, causing some scandal when political pressure was applied to the press who all tried to cover the story. They managed to stop the news spreading but Ronnie was advised to back off from his relationship.

Mike was now confident enough to have a quiet word about his concerns about Ronnie to Reggie. He never learnt what happened between the brothers who were increasingly being recognised as psychotic, but Ronnie made no further approaches to him. By now Mike was a key member of The Firm. He managed their protection rackets, had been involved in four armed robberies, and was increasingly seen as the leader of The Firm in the Krays' absence.

But Ronnie was by now being increasingly recognised for extremes in his mental illness often resulting in violence. He took particular offence to being supposedly called 'a fat poofter, by Richard Hart, a member of the Richardson gang.' This culminated with him going into London's Blind Beggar pub and shooting Richard dead in full public view.

Then in 1968 Detective Chief Superintendent 'Nipper' Reed of Scotland Yard achieved his most critical mission. He arrested the twins for murder and other criminal activities. The following year the Kray twins were convicted and a life sentence with a minimum term of 30 years was imposed, they were both only thirty-six years old. Now they asked Mike, even at his very young age of twenty-four, to take over all The Firm's affairs. Mike had kept himself in really good shape through regular exercise, he was married and had no sexual interest at all in men. His family and his work were his main priorities. His wife, Fiona, and their, by now, four children took up a lot of Mike's time and attention.

He was therefore in the prime of life to take over and become London's most feared and respected gangster. But, as he grew up, he had also been very carefully observing the way Ronnie and Reggie went about their business and carefully learnt from the mistakes they made. In his opinion both were violent psychopaths, they loved violence for its own sake. They also held rigidly to their own rather peculiar set of values. These were that their mother, Violet, was the most important person in their life. To them she was literally a goddess. They controlled The Firm mercilessly. Anyone out of order was severely punished. They had murdered seven fellow criminals that Mike knew of; in each case they froze the body, then dismembered and burned the corpse, therefore leaving no evidence.

The twins also were very generous and popular with the local people. They gave significant sums of money to old folks' homes and local charities, also were very generous at their clubs and pubs with hospitality. But they absolutely detested the drugs trade, which was becoming very important across the country and particularly in London. The Firm as they were called stated in no uncertain terms, they would have absolutely nothing to do with it. They regarded it as an evil trade.

Mike completely disagreed with the twins. But now, with them safely locked in prison, he gradually forced his way in, and took over other criminals' trade in drugs. It wasn't long before he was in control of drugs in the East End and in other parts of London. Reggie died in prison in 1995 aged sixty-two. Ronnie was released from prison in the year 2000 on compassionate grounds, then eight weeks later died from bladder cancer. Both criminals had massive funerals in London, attended by huge crowds of cockneys.

Now the whole business was unquestionably Mike's. He was a very powerful, seemingly unassailable figure. He withdrew himself from personal involvement in the criminal acts he had The Firm commit and became a very popular London socialite.

Now it was time to begin. David taxied to the garage and dressed in his posh outfit. Then he drove the ambulance and parked it round a couple of corners from the nightclub where Big Mike used to meet with his fellow gangsters. It was a smart place, very popular with minor film stars and other supposed celebs. Even Mike's fellow thugs dressed up for their regular Thursday evening which would end with many drinks into the wee small hours. David entered carrying in his pocket a little bottle of the knockout drops. He had practised over and over again how to conceal the bottle, then leaning across, opened his fist, allowing the liquid to fall into his target's glass.

David moved up the bar and, standing close to where Mike was holding court, leant over as if to catch the barmaid's eye. Then, looking as if he was affected by alcohol, he released a dose into Mike's glass. He had however drunk nothing. Every drink he had ordered and paid for went into a nearby flower vase. He didn't have any problems stumbling and apologising just as one of Mike's mates leapt to hit him, since he had obviously had too much to drink. But the deed was done.

David staggered out of the nightclub and went round to where the ambulance stood. He donned the red moustache, beard, wig and his driver's outfit then drove back round the corners. As he travelled, he listened into the emergency service until he heard the call for an ambulance from the nightclub. He turned on the siren and flashing lights and screeched to a halt. His only fear had been that a real ambulance might arrive. So, in the ten minutes he had waited David made three emergency calls requesting an ambulance in different and faraway places. It all went like clockwork.

David had no sooner pulled up when three of the thugs carried Mike out of the club and told him to lift their boss into the ambulance. The head bodyguard was a huge guy called Jimmy. He insisted on coming with Mike but he was told firmly that that was not allowed, but if you wish to grab a taxi, knowing that they'd had far too much drink to risk driving, they would find Mike in the emergency ward of a local hospital which he named. Then he roared off direct to his garage.

He knew the drugs would soon begin to wear off. Mike made little resistance as David gagged him, then bound him with the zip ties into the chair. Then he was pushed in and locked in the van. David left his driver's costume in the ambulance and dressed in the denim jacket and jeans. Then he drove out and securely locked the garage door. He made his way north of the capital onto the M11. It would take between one and a half and two hours to reach his hideout. Every hour he stopped the ambulance on the hard shoulder and gave Mike another injection. He had been told the dose lasted for at least an hour, certainly the cumulative effect seemed to hit him hard and Mike seemed out for the count.

Mike slowly came to, but when he tried to move, he found that he was firmly secured to the metal chair he was in. Then he realised with shock that he was not only naked but a circular hole had been cut and lined in the seat of the chair, therefore his private parts dangled down. He also had some kind of hood over his head. There was a slit on the front of it for his eyes but his mouth was gagged.

His victim tried rocking the wheelchair to move it but it was secured as firmly as a rock to the floor. The room was in total darkness and there was not even a sound. He tried to cry out, that just made a slight muffled grunt, nevertheless it was enough to trigger the video camera and sound recording observing him. After about half an hour, a door opened behind him. A very bright light was switched on, pointed directly into his eyes blinding him. Someone ripped the tape away from his mouth and pulled the hood off. He spat out coarsely 'Who the fuck are you? You bastard! You have no fucking idea the pain you are going to suffer before you die in agony! The only—' Mike reeled back into the chair as he was stunned twice with the gun.

The only response was that a sheet of paper was held before him just to the side of the light. He read it with increasing horror.

It said in block capitals:

'Shut up scum, and read. Your threats mean nothing to me. No-one knows where you are, far away from London, neither your family nor any of your thugs have a clue what happened to you, nor where to find you. We are in a very isolated area. Even if you scream your filthy head off no one will hear you. The reason you are here is because your time as a kingpin of your horrible drugs trade is at an end as from now.

You will have a few days to consider your position. You can crap and piss as much as you want. You will only increase the stink of your fear. A water hose has been secured on your right; I will leave it on a trickle. You can reach it with your mouth. I will not have you starving. Ready-made meals will be positioned in front of your mouth. They will start when I believe you're ready to listen. You can be here for months, it's totally up to you. What I want from you is the following:

1. a list of your suppliers, details of how shipments are made and when due.

2. a list of those key thugs you supply with contact details.
3. at the end of your period here, a solemn promise which I shall record of you swearing never to have anything to do with drugs for the rest of your miserable life.
4. Finally, a payment of £200,000 will be made by you directly into my bank account.
5. If I ever find you've broken your promise at any time, or should you try to evade paying the monies due, I will kill you, nothing is more certain than that.

'Now, do you take any important medication?'

'What the fuck's that got to do with you, you bastard, as soon as I get out of this chair no medicine in the world will ever help you—' Big Mike reeled back at the brief burst from the stun gun.

When he came to he heard, 'Just shut your stinking mouth, scum, any more of that I will turn the water off, and knock you out completely' Mike heard the lighting being switched off, the door behind him opened, and someone left. He was once again back in the darkness. Mike tried to stem his growing panic. After all he, Mike, was one of London's most feared villains, but how the hell was he going to get out of this? Who the hell is this bastard, is he just in it for the money?'

The next day, mid-morning, the door opened again, the light was switched on, dazzling him, and then moved to the side to highlight the sheet of paper. The same disguised voice demanded, 'Now tell me, do you take any important medication?'

'Yes, you bugger. I take a blood thinner and three pills for cholesterol protection?'

'Does your wife know where they are?'

'Yes.'

A hand appeared holding a mobile phone to Mike's ear. 'When she replies say nothing of this otherwise you will be stunned again. Do not answer any her questions. Just say

“Fiona, tell nobody I phoned. If you do, I’ll be in real danger. Just get my meds from the bathroom cabinet. Then at 7 o’clock tonight, drive to the phone box on the corner of Broadway and Laburnam Grove. You’ll be told what to do then”.’

Fiona drove her sports car to the callbox. She left Mike’s medicines on the passenger seat and went in. The phone rang. She picked it up and with difficulty heard a garbled voice say, ‘Now, Mike’s wife, drive on for just over three quarters of a mile, you will then see a parking area on your left, Drive in, leave the package of medicines and go immediately home. Now Fiona, tell nobody about this, or your husband will be in danger.’

‘But what’s happening, where is he—’ The phone was dead.

David watched her drive towards him. He used his night vision binoculars to check that she was alone in the car as far as he could see, and that there was no one following her. When she dropped the package and drove off, David emerged from his hiding place in the trees. He took the package then turned his motorbike onto a narrow forest track which would lead him onto the main road heading north.

Mike was very concerned when David gave him his drugs. ‘What about Fiona? If you’ve touched a hair on her head I will—’

When he once more came to David said, ‘Now look, Mike, surely by now you realise your position is absolutely helpless. Of course I haven’t harmed Fiona, I leave that behaviour to lowlife like you. Now, how’s about it, are you ready to at last tell me what I want?’

It took just two more days of drugs torture and sleep deprivation before Mike admitted defeat. But late one night he said, ‘Look, man. I have had about enough. If this goes on much longer, I will be seriously ill. Tell me again what it is you want from me.’

David set up his recording equipment and sat back enthralled, as Mike revealed all.

# Chapter 8

# Birmingham

David decided to follow exactly the same plan and use the same methods as had worked so well in London to bribe and threaten his way up the drugs ladder.

The only useful information Mike had managed to give David was that the most important criminal in Birmingham was an ex-Nigerian whose name was Debare. David booked into a Travelodge close to where most African immigrants had made their homes. He soon found out from_prostitutes who he made contact with the name of another African. This man had come from Somalia, and was a dealer in drugs. David found to his pleasure that unlike London, torture was not necessary; money alone would give him the information he sought.

It only cost £400 which he thought was a very good deal. But it turned out that the Somalian had experienced some bad times with the city's drugs criminals so was only too eager to help with anything that might damage them.

He learnt that Debare had arrived after fleeing Africa some seven years previously. He initially set up business with his brother Tayo who had been a small time criminal in the city for a long time. But it did not take Debare much time before he was leading what soon became a very powerful gang. At first it was all about shop lifting and burglary then it was onto armed robbery, protection rackets and running prostitutes but soon drugs became the priority.

The dealer told as much as he knew about Debare and his gang which included that they were seen regularly at a big night club which he thought they might own and run. Then he told David the name of a guy who had fallen out with Debare, hated him deeply and might have more information.

David arranged to meet the thug in a pub of his choice.

He offered the guy money for information about Debare and his crimes. The man, a huge, fat, muscular black guy grabbed him by the collar, and spat into his face yelling 'What do you want with that fucker? He is my enemy for life.' David said that he was a writer working on a book about criminals selling drugs. When the man realised that David could damage the man he hated, he was only too ready to tell everything he knew, especially when David greased his palm with £20 notes.

David learnt that the headman in the drugs scene in the city was from Nigeria. His name was Debare Okoye and he and his growing family lived not far from the hotel David was lodged in. This time the gangster had not bought a large mansion in the gentrified suburbs of Birmingham but had decided to live centrally and openly amongst his gang members and some of his dealers. However, instead of living in one of the small flats in the area Debare owned a whole block of them. He and his family and at least four of his gangsters with their families lived in the same block.

Debare was now heading for sixty years old. His name meant 'one who came from good times'. That hardly applied to Debare's life story. He swore at the end of his time in Nigeria that he would never have anything to do with guns again as long as he lived. He was more than breaking that promise as soon as he arrived in England.

His country, Nigeria, had been a restless, at times violent place, up until 1960 when they gained independence from their colonial masters, Great Britain. Like most of his countrymen he hoped this new world would bring in a period of peace and prosperity. The opposite turned out to be the case. After only six years the religious suppression and terrorism of Debare's people's Christian faith became overwhelming and they fled to the east where their own people were the dominant population.

They were led by Lt. Col. Ojokwi who persuaded them to establish an independent country, the Republic of Biafra.

But no matter how intensive the diplomatic negotiations were, war broke out between the two countries. The Nigerian superior military forces soon were having success upon success against Debare's own army. In 1970 Orwerri, the provincial capital of Biafra, was taken by the Nigerians. Four days later Biafra surrendered to Nigeria. Once again Debare and his fellow Christians were subjected to appalling cruelty and savagery by the Moslem soldiers.

The terrible incident that finished off Debare was when he was called out to the nearby Nunnery. Nigerian soldiers had raped and mutilated all of the nuns. The place was just a terrible scene of blood-soaked horror. This was the final straw. Debare decided he would leave his country and go and seek work and employment with his brother Tayo who was living in a place called Birmingham in England. He took with him his wife and his three children; the middle child was a lad named Amandi. He was only six years old so grew up to go to school in Birmingham, learned and spoke English and soon grew up to know and feel nothing of his childhood in Africa.

Debare's brother Tayo was a small time criminal in one of England's biggest industrial cities. So Amandi grew up in a tough area to a tough childhood. Youngsters did try to bully him at school but soon found out that he was more than capable of looking after himself and had a vicious temper when aroused. He was always involved in scuffles and fights and became well respected by his fellow pupils. His father, spotting his potential, first used him to suss out the properties he was planning to rob, then having taught Amandi the necessary skills, went on to how to break into the houses himself and what to steal.

Debare was absolutely ruthless in his dealings with his fellow criminals. On one occasion he tortured a fellow criminal so badly that the man died. Debare was pleasantly surprised to find out just how he enjoyed killing. From then on his reputation just grew bigger and bigger until eventually he was running the drugs scene in the city.

Amandi's father, Debare, was now the very highly

respected leader of the two main gangs in Birmingham, the Burger Boys and the 61 Gang. Their only real opposition came from the Manchester underworld. The drugs trade in that city had been under the control of three long established thugs but now it was led by two violent criminals,_Thomas and Raymond Petty, who had built the most vicious and feared of the gangs, The Pitt Bull Crew. And, although Thomas had recently started a 30-year prison sentence, that had not stopped Raymond turning their main activity into the very lucrative trade in heroin.

Just the previous month another of the leaders had been caught. He was stopped by the police and his vehicle searched. About 4 kg of heroin were confiscated and the man sent to prison. Manchester police’s drugs squad had formed a very effective team of officers from their own force and with members of the National Crime Agency, the NCA. Their mission was to destroy Manchester's growing drug trade. They were starting to have real success and this latest arrest led to two more gang leaders being arrested and sentenced to a long time in prison for drugs offences.

The new leadership started looking elsewhere as the Manchester police were getting just too successful for their liking. So where else to sell the large quantity of imported heroin they had amassed? Birmingham with its overcrowded, run-down suburbs and thriving drugs scene seemed ideal.

A meeting was arranged in a Birmingham nightclub between three senior gangsters from Manchester who met Debare, his brother in one of the city’s best restaurants, Tayo, and another of his key men, Nasha.

Debare was only too well aware of the success the police had been having and the damage they had caused to the Manchester drug business. So the last thing he wanted was to have them turn their attentions onto him and his gang. Also, his own trade in drugs was going extremely well, thanks very much, so although he was offered a sizeable cut of heroin sales if the two gangs joined together, the Manchester trade was just too risky, so was refused.

When they offered to increase the percentage share of

heroin profits and grew quite hostile, Debare told them to fuck off back to Manchester. In a furious temper they left, vowing that this would not the end of their efforts in Birmingham.

It took them just seven weeks until, after a number of sizeable bribes backed up with threats of torture, Nasha decided to change allegiance providing he was offered the leading position in the joint gang trade in Birmingham.

Nasha let the Manchester men know about one of Debare's regular, secret habits, this was a weekly evening spent having a massage and you can imagine what else with one of the prostitutes who looked after customers at his own nightclub. The woman named Flo answered a knock on her door, assuming it was Debare although he was a bit early for his usual session. Two masked gunmen grabbed her, then tied her up and gagged her. It was not long before Debare arrived, used his own key to enter Flo's flat and made his way into the bedroom. The door slammed shut behind him and a big man wearing a mask shot him in the chest with a silenced gun. A second shot to finish Debare off was then fired into his head.

When Amandi arrived at the nightclub having been told of this, the place was in uproar. Nasha held a pistol to his head and yelled out to the assembled thugs, 'Right, it's all over now. Debare is dead and I am now taking over from him. I will be selling heroin from our new friends in Manchester. Anyone who wants no part of this leave now but be aware that you are passing up the chance of making a sizeable fortune.'

Amandi looked at him and said, 'So you've got what you've always wanted, Nasha. But to be honest I was getting a bit fed up with the way things were going here. I fell out with my father years ago. The loyal son you've all seen was an act. I didn't think much of the way he was leading our work and I could not believe why he turned down a great chance to work with the Manchester gangs. So put your gun away Nasha, I'm in, I'm with you.'

Amandi let things go on for a few months, all the time

observing everything that was happening and learning all the time about the new trade. Then, just before Christmas, he learnt of a planned celebration. A grand dinner between Nasha's men and the leaders from Manchester.

The members' only dining club was on the top floor of the casino they owned. The large room was lavishly decorated and the long dining table gleamed with candle light. The table was set out for the eighteen invitees whose silver cutlery glistened, as did the crystal glasses.

After Nasha had welcomed all his guests, he clapped his hands and from the rear door strolled a line of scantily clad, female beauties. 'Gentlemen, we have got on extremely well and have very good cause to celebrate our work over the past few months. I thought this would be a very appropriate final course this evening.' The young ladies sauntered out as a roar of drink fuelled laughter erupted.

As the men settled down to enjoy the luxurious banquet to come, a dinner-suited waiter scurried over to Nasha. He handed him a message marked with his name and stating:

**URGENT.**

Nasha's face turned a very pale white as he tried to take on board what the message said:

**'Right, bastard, your time has come at last. You murdered my beloved father and betrayed all your colleagues in Birmingham. Now payback is due. It is time for you and these bastards from Manchester to get what you all so thoroughly deserve.'**

In his office on the ground floor, Amandi pressed the electric detonator. The charges exploded from the slabs of very powerful plastic explosive he had screwed into the underside of the dining room table at regular intervals. The resulting explosion not only obliterated the assembled gangsters but started a dramatic, all-consuming blaze. Amandi quietly made his way down to the rear door, his own private exit. He went into his limousine and was driven home, exalting.

Amandi now felt that it was his responsibility to look after the family and what was now his gang.

So many of the leaders of the gangs in both Manchester and Birmingham had been killed that Amandi had little difficulty in establishing himself as the head of the underworld in Birmingham but now also in Manchester. Apart from London, Amandi was probably now the most powerful gangster in the land.

This was the man David had chosen to take on! Amandi's reputation for extreme violence, as well as carrying out horribly painful tortures, and his heavy involvement with drugs made him just the ideal target for his next mission.

David considered renting a flat in the road opposite to where Amandi lived but concluded that a white face would stand out far too noticeably in that immigrant area. So instead he stayed in his room in the Travelodge and flew his drone to a rooftop opposite his target's home. He sat watching the drone's recording as the Nigerian strolled out into the waiting BMW with his guard. Even three stories up it was easy to hear the rap music belting from the car at full volume. He made the drone lift off and follow the car to a large nightclub in the downtown area. This was the one he had been notified was likely to be owned by Amandi and was one of Birmingham's best-known locations for those desperate to buy any kind of drug.

Once he'd established that this was a twice weekly routine, David, donning his posh businessman's outfit of smart suit, darkened moustache and gelled hair, started going to the club. There was no colour bar of course and there was more than one wealthy looking, white man drinking alcohol before heading for the gambling tables. At pretty much the same time every evening, about 11 o'clock, Amandi and his bodyguard Chigbo, would emerge from the private office on the top floor above the casino. No doubt there were closed-circuit TV cameras there so they could watch everything that was going on, all of the action at the gambling tables.

Amandi and his thug always went over to the bar, chatted to the attractive blonde bar lady. She already had the cork loosened in the magnum of vintage champagne he obviously enjoyed. It was his regular tipple.

Sitting up on his own high stool, Amandi would sip his champagne while his gambling pit=bosses came to make brief reports of how things were going. He took little notice of the half-sozzled businessmen in a smart suit, a typical loser, who was standing at the bar beside him. The man kept leaning over trying to catch the barmaid's eye. Neither she, Amandi, nor his bodyguard, saw the hand briefly hover and release the drug into Amandi's glass.

The drunk gave up trying to get service and left the nightclub.

About ten minutes later Amandi started to feel very dizzy, slumped forward and fell off his stool. Chigbo dashed forward, thrust the casino workers aside and checked his boss's pulse. It felt fine, what the hell was this? He dialled 999 on his mobile and asked for an ambulance, then he and two of the bar staff shouldered the boss through the crowds to and out of the main door.

After only about another ten minutes they heard a siren and an ambulance with flashing lights screeched to a halt in front of them. The driver, wearing a uniform jacket came over, checked Amandi's pulse, then used a probe to test the oxygen levels in his blood.

'What the hell's wrong with the boss?' questioned Chigbo.

'I don't know, his pulse is okay there's nothing I can find wrong. He needs to get to hospital quickly to be properly checked out.'

'OK I'm coming with him, Chigbo,' said in a voice which brooked no argument.

'Right if you insist but you shouldn't be here.' They lifted Amandi onto the wheelchair and pushed it up the ramp. His bodyguard sat on the bench opposite as the ambulance took off fast, this time without the siren blaring.

After a short distance the ambulance came to a halt, the rear door opened and the driver entered saying, ‘Time for me to check out how my patient’s doing.’ Chigbo watched carefully as the man checked out Amandi as before then he gasped as the driver drew a weird looking gun from his rear belt, pointed it at him and without a word fired it into him. Chigbo just felt a stunning, shuddering blow then he collapsed. David dragged the heavy body with difficulty out into the quiet alleyway he'd reversed into.

Using his syringe David injected a dose of the drug into Chigbo’s neck, closed up the ambulance and drove off heading in a south-easterly direction. Eventually he joined the M6 and made his way cross country then onto the smaller roads until eventually the ambulance drove into the garage of the farmhouse.

David secured the ambulance in the garage, opened its rear door, pulled down the ramp and pushed Amandi in the wheelchair out of the garage. He locked it securely and took his captive into the house. He went into the downstairs bathroom and shoved the wheelchair into the shower cabinet. Carefully turning it, he secured it to the rag bolts and tightened them down firmly. So that he could at last get some well-earned rest, David gave Amandi another injection. It was nearly 3 a.m. and David was knackered, so he went to bed and fell into a very deep sleep.

At six the following morning, prompted by his phone alarm, David dressed then went into the bathroom and set the shower to cold and turned it on full. Amandi was shocked awake. He yelled at the top of his voice as soon as his tormentor had ripped the sticky tape from across his mouth. David filmed his outburst recording him as he screeched filthier upon filthier insults and threatened unmentionable terrors and pain to his kidnapper.

‘Right, you piece of filth, I am going to explain exactly what your position really is and tell you what I intend to do with you. I can be persuaded to agree to let you extend the miserable, disgusting life with the rest of your fellow scum, however death is always close at hand.'

No one, but no one had ever dared speak to Amandi in this way. Swearing foully he was about to tell David of the hell that awaited him when his torturer took out the stun gun and sent him back into semi-unconsciousness on his seat.

'Now you stupid bastard, that just gives you a taste of what will happen if you open your dirty mouth again, unless is to say something I want to hear. Do you understand me?'

The Nigerian just swore again so David gave him another short burst from the stun gun.

When he came to, David asked, 'Now, do you understand me?' Amandi nodded angrily but didn't speak. David gave him a bit of time to properly come to, then said, 'We can keep going like this as long as you want. Me, I've got all the time in the world and more than enough charges for my gun then you could ever cope with. Now, you sad fart, for once in your life, try to listen.' David took out a sheet of paper and pinned it onto the door facing Amandi. 'This, scum, is my list of demands. You have three days of pain and suffering before I will ask you once again if you accept it. In the meantime, here's a taste of what you're in for.'

Amandi looked on in horror as David took a set of battery charging leads which were connected to the mains and clicked each one onto one of his balls. 'Now, when I press this switch, Amandi, your balls will receive an electric shock. The longer I press it for, the more painful it will be. By the end of three days you will not only be writhing in agony but your balls will be burnt to a crisp. I will then fasten it elsewhere to your body. I leave it to your fertile imagination to work out where that might be. I'll just give you a taste of it.' He turned on the charger.

Amandi felt a tingle then an extremely painful electric shock running through his nether regions. 'Please stop,' he screamed. David turned the charger off.

'That's better, that's a bit more of the kind of language I expect to hear from you. I'll be back in two hours' time to give you another dose. In the meantime, think carefully. There is no escape, no one knows you are here. This is a secret hideout which nobody is aware of.

'Now you are here, you are completely at my mercy. Apart from the first three days of unmitigated pain I will continue with worse and more evil torture until I get what I want or until your worthless body is dead in the wheelchair. Do you understand?'

All he got was an angry cry. 'Right, you fucking bastard.'

Amandi was a very different captive to Big Mike. He proved much harder to break down. Ever since his youth he had kept himself extremely physically fit and David found him mentally strong as well. But no one could last more than a few days in such surroundings and in such pain. Amandi was confined in a nasty, smelly box subjected to regular pain, frequent stunning and repeated doses of drugs. So most of the time he was either out or semi-conscious in agony. On the couple of occasions that he dared to hurl foul insults again at David the charger was turned back on causing severe pain.

It took however eight days of this form of torture and suffering before the Nigerian finally gave up. David sat entranced as the man submitted and described those who were his supposed pals, his gang members. Amandi told everything. All about who the drugs were bought from, how they were obtained, who his dealers were. In fact, told him everything David wanted to know. He laid out in detail the makeup of his gang and told about the youngsters they were now recruiting to supply and sell drugs outside Birmingham.

David dressed his shattered victim, then drove him in the builder's van to a deserted municipal car park just beside Amandi's home. There he left him curled up by the entrance. On his way back, he phoned Chigbo at the night club to tell him where he could find his boss. Now it was time to head north.

# Chapter 9

## The Daily Mail

David had now reached the point where it was time to make contact with the national press. David needed to find a reliable source, a senior crime reporter who could pass on information about the drugs trade and likely targets but also would be ready to receive information he gleaned from the gangsters and use it for publication in articles or perhaps a book to result in damaging effects to this evil drugs trade. He thought his best bet was that popular newspaper the *Daily Mail*. Looking on the Internet under Daily Mail crime, there were a number of men named including the boss of the reporting team but David had concluded that a female reporter might be more sympathetic to his cause. Ah here we are, Roberta Harvey, senior reporter. He researched under her name and liked very much the style of her writing and reporting. She had been with the *Mail* for well over seven years and had written up some very serious crimes.

David telephoned the *Mail's* London head office and asked to speak to Roberta only to be told, 'Sorry, she's out in the case just now, can somebody else help?'

'No thank you, it's Roberta herself I need to speak to. Can you please pass a message to her?' 'Certainly.'

The message left on her desk read, 'Roberta, could you please telephone Alan Carter on 07740 678276. He says he has something which will be of definite interest to the newspaper and to yourself.'

Just after 8 a.m. the next morning, David's mobile rang. 'Hello, hello, is that Alan Carter?'

'Speaking.'

'Hello Alan, this is Roberta Harvey of the *Daily Mail*. You left me an intriguing message. How can I help?'

'Thanks for phoning back, Roberta. I am working on a project which will lead to a major story about the drugs trade in this country. Could we arrange to meet somewhere quiet to talk things through, maybe for a lunch or dinner and I will tell you all about it?'

'Well Alan, I'm solidly booked today, how's about lunch tomorrow, any idea where?'

'No, this is almost foreign country to me, Roberta, it's very much your own patch. Could you please choose a restaurant that you like, how's about 12.30?'

The pair met in Sabatini's Italian restaurant. David was very pleasantly surprised to see how attractive the reporter was. Roberta was slim, just under his own height, with glinting black eyes, and dark hair which would have done a Colleen proud. She was dressed in a smart casual way, in a denim skirt, colourful blouse and a tweed jacket that fitted her very neatly.

Roberta meanwhile was sizing up her potential new source. He had a very pleasant, attractive, soft Scottish accent, maybe from the Highlands. Alan had short reddish hair a tache and a beard of similar colour. He was dressed in a blue cashmere sweater and smart, but casual trousers. She instantly liked him, but thought the little beard and tache didn't do him any favours at all.

After they had ordered their meal, Roberta said, 'Okay, tell me your story. I am intrigued?'

'How's about waiting until we've enjoyed our meal and just use the time to get to know one another, Roberta?'

'Alan, no way, I am very keen to hear what you have to say. I promise I won't speak with my mouth full, but will listen to you very carefully.'

'Okay and by the way Roberta, just to be clear, this meal's on me please. Right, I am a published author but without much success to date. The name I gave you is false, as is the moustache and beard that I saw you looking at. For very important and personal reasons which you will understand as I go on, I need to use a fake ID and would ask you to please keep this discussion totally confidential, for your ears only.'

'I have a very strong motivation to carry out a

programme of vengeance against the drugs barons, particularly those who you have written about who are in control of what you have called county lines. They are a very evil extension of the drugs trade to young kids.'

'My campaign, which I am now prepared to begin, is designed to strike terror into the scum involved in the trade right across the country.'

'Are you alone, have you anybody who is working with you? Have you any conception of the risks, the terrible danger you're putting yourself in?'

'Roberta, if I were to tell you my full story, you would soon realise that my own life has become of very little worth to me. No matter what you say or do, even if you're not interested at all, there is nothing going to stop me carrying out my campaign.'

'OK, Alan, tell me as much as you can, particularly what drove you to start this campaign.'

'As part of my work, I have already identified a number of key players in some of the main cities. My plan is to select a small number of them, capture them, and take them as my prisoner to a discrete hideaway. There I will use threats, drugs and if necessary, torture, to find out all they know about the business.

'All my planning and preparation has been carefully recorded. All actions from now on will be noted, filmed and either recorded there and then or transferred onto computer files. At the end of my campaign, which I estimate will take most of this year, a full copy of all of these recordings including films of my victims' confessions will be handed to you by me at a future meeting to be arranged.'

'My God, Alan, have you any idea, even the slightest conception of what you're getting into?'

'Yes, Roberta, and I'm fully prepared to risk all to achieve my objectives. As you can only too well imagine, this will be a hell of an exclusive story for you, and there will inevitably be a bestselling book to come out of it all.'

'Bloody hell, Alan, why me? Of all the reporters you could have chosen, why did you select me?'

‘It’s very simple, Roberta, I've read and thoroughly enjoyed your reports, their concise writing, they seem accurate and very much to the point. I like your style and the content.’

‘Okay, let's get down to brass tacks. How much money are you looking for?’

‘I do not want any payment, Roberta. My return will be the huge damage your articles, the subsequent publicity, and the book will do to this evil, pernicious trade.’

‘So what is it specifically that you’re looking for at this stage from me?’

‘I would like as much information as you can let me have on the key figures in the drugs trade centred on the following British cities – London, Southampton, Derby, Birmingham, Manchester, Newcastle, Carlisle, Glasgow, Aberdeen, Edinburgh and Dundee. I will select a small number of these depending on the quality of the information you can get for me.’

After they said farewell, a stunned Roberta walked slowly back to her office.

She sat at her desk, quietly ruminating over what had been said. It was obvious that Alan or whatever his real name was, had suffered terribly from the criminals in the drugs trade. She felt heart sorry for the man, and all that he had been through, and well understood why he was embarking on this most risky venture. Roberta decided, as Alan had asked, to keep the story to herself just now, but no matter what he said she would try to find out who he really was and what tragedy had driven him down this road.

The only clues she had were that he was definitely Scottish, probably a Highlander, and his family had probably been severely damaged by drugs in the near past probably resulting in a death or deaths. She would make a start by looking over the history of recent drugs crimes in Scotland's three main cities, Glasgow, Edinburgh and Aberdeen. She also carefully checked out records of deaths linked to drugs.

In the meantime, Roberta's main work was extremely

demanding. As levels of crime, particularly those involving violence in the capital, soared. She was so busy reporting that she had little time for her detective work. In fact, she was usually completely knackered by the time she got home, not capable of telephoning or working in the computer anymore.

# Chapter 10

# Edinburgh

Colin Stevenson had probably the finest body of all David's captives; he was extremely fit for his age.

His fitness was almost solely due to his work exercising and fighting in the karate ring. Whilst at school he had met Saburo, a young lad from the outskirts of Tokyo, and a recent arrival to the school. Colin was one of the very few pupils to make the lad welcome.

Saburo's father, Nakia, had been over the moon at his latest posting. He had been appointed translator to the Japanese embassy in Scotland's capital city. Nakia was a keen student of history and especially had become fascinated with that of Scotland, particularly the very romantic and glamorous tales built around the time of Bonnie Prince Charlie, the Young Pretender, in the mid-1700s.

Nakia's wife actually feared he was becoming infatuated. He had paid money to have the family name somehow transcribed into a Scottish clan of his own making. Then of course Saburo and the rest of the family were forced to wear a kilt on social occasions. Saburo however refused point-blank to wear it to school. He was getting jeered and bullied enough as things were. Saburo had certainly not received much of the welcome to foreigners which he had been told was typically Scottish. From his fellow pupils, one gang especially were picking on him all the time, they were led by a tough cookie called Willie. So Saburo was extremely happy when Colin introduced himself and welcomed the Japanese youngster into the school.

Colin said he was interested in Japan and in particular in learning about their national sport of karate. Like many Japanese youngsters, Saburo had been required from just over four years old to learn the basics of this martial art. By now he was an advanced fighter heading towards his black belt, the expert qualification. He was only too pleased to take Colin along to his class and introduce him to his Sensei. It was not long before the two lads would often be found practising after class. Colin was himself a tough youngster, very capable of looking after himself. Soon Willie had learnt to have nothing to do at all to do with this pair. They were to be feared and respected as fighters.

Things however greatly improved when Colin took Willie aside one day and said, 'Why were you making things so unpleasant for Saburo? What the hell do you have against him? He's a youngster, a foreigner in our city. We should be offering him friendship, not insults.' All became clear when Willie explained that his grandfather, Alec, had been a prisoner of war, first in Burma then in Japan. He was treated incredibly cruelly, horribly by the Japanese guards who looked down on men they captured as cowards, not fit to wear a soldier's uniform. When they had a living God on earth, their emperor. Alec had in fact worked on the famous railway of death in Burma.

After being told this Saburo said to Willie he wanted a word. He listened to the story then to Willie's surprise told him that his own father, Nakia, was very against the Japanese military's actions in those times. He was in despair of what they had done in the name of his country towards their prisoners of war. One of his jobs in the embassy, when meeting others, was to try to explain that there was another, much more pleasant side to the Japanese character. That now things had improved hugely. From then on Willie became one of their friends.

Willie asked if he could come along to the karate class and was made very welcome. He too was a tough lad and was soon mastering the early stages of karate very well. In fact, the three of them became a team as the club travelled not just in Scotland but in England as well, having contests with karate clubs all over the place. They developed a very high reputation for their skills and their Sensei grew extremely proud of his three kilted warriors. He named them thus because Saburo had reluctantly agreed to wear his kilt when going to the contests and persuaded both Colin and Willie to do the same.

Colin was the third child to be born to his father Kenny and his wife Ellen. Kenny himself was a member of the karate club but was not particularly good, nor keen on the sport. He was more interested in learning to fight and take care of himself. This was because he was a petty gangster who had graduated from being involved in violence on the back streets to running a group of ladies for hire. Then, like many of Scotland's criminals, Kenny turned his attention to selling drugs. He started off dealing in cannabis and LSD then progressed onto some of the stronger drugs which were becoming more readily available throughout the whole country.

Kenny had never got on very well with his son, Colin. But recently, had asked him to help out with his drug dealings in areas outside his own patch in Edinburgh. Colin was not keen in any way to become part of this criminal trade, but the money was far too good to resist. So he was soon regularly missing out on his karate weekends and travelling to places like Broxburn and Newton around Edinburgh, selling drugs and building up a network of suppliers. Colin was soon as well-known as Kenny. It was funny how quickly things progressed from him dealing with small packets of drugs, showing his fellow schoolmates how to sniff lines of the white powder from the backs of their hands in the boys' toilets at school, to trips travelling around the central belt of Scotland making himself known. Colin didn't take any notice of Mr Cafferty, his sports teacher, warning all of the pupils about the dangers of drugs and not to be tempted even to try them out.

Then things changed hugely. Kenny was arrested by the police. They had been following him for some time and knew pretty much all about his trade in drugs. But they knew little about his up-and-coming son's reputation. They thought he was too young to be in involved in anything more than minor offences at school. So Colin took over the business in Edinburgh and it soon grew from strength to strength. They started coming up against some of the other gangs who were extremely annoyed at people trying to intrude on their trade. They had although learnt of Colin's reputation and at times had seen his karate skills put to good work. As some of their own gangsters were disabled, sometimes permanently, when they tried to take him down.

Colin was doing a lot of business for and on behalf of the most powerful dealer in Edinburgh, a violent thug called Derek Flynn. He had been around the city's underworld for many years. This man saw a lot of himself in Colin and offered to take him on board as second-in-command of his own empire.

Derek now asked a big favour of Colin. He had been very concerned about his daughter Debbie. She had fallen in with a bit of a bad lot at school. What amazing cheek even to think in these terms considering his own background! But he asked Colin whether she could join the karate club. Debbie was not mustard keen, not at all, to learn and apply karate but she also took a real liking to Colin, who by now was not only super fit but very good-looking.

The two of them got on extremely well which Derek was delighted to see. He too had come to really like, but more importantly respect Colin, and was over the moon to think his beloved daughter might find true happiness with him.

The following year Debbie and Colin announced their engagement and were wed in the next year. Derek couldn't believe his good fortune. Not only at his daughter's choice of husband, but he had never in all his life seen her look so happy and fulfilled. He thought his happiness could never be better until the night when Colin sat him down, placed his favourite drink in front of him and told him that he and Debbie were expecting their much wanted, and his much desired, first grandchild.

Derek ran his empire from a private suite of offices and meeting rooms in Musselburgh race course. This is established as one of the UK's most stylish race courses. He not only ran the racing ground and employed all the staff but was heavily involved in the betting, including fixing the odds as he desired. However, delighted as he was with the news about his daughter's future, Derek knew, but did not tell Debbie nor her new husband that his health was really beginning to fail. He had long-standing problems with both heart and kidneys and was having to pay a lot of money for extra specialist investigation. His empire was by now being run totally by Colin. Not only was he now seen as Edinburgh's drug baron but also the main man for Perth and Dundee to the north and Berwick-upon-Tweed to the south. The English border certainly presented no barrier to the up-and-coming drugs trade.

Colin not only inherited Derek's business, he also took over responsibility for the head bodyguard, an immense, tough Irishman named Bob, but who everyone knew by his last name, Cafferty.

David had read all this background information. He had visited the racecourse, enquired politely about Derek's health at the hospital, visited both Colin and Debbie's lovely home in Polmont, and her father's mansion in Saughtonhall. He also found out that Derek did not have long to live so all his energies could be concentrated on Colin.

David waited for a particular Saturday, a major event in the horse racing calendar. He knew that most of Colin's main gang would congregate at Musselborough. Dressed in casual clothes he approached a young waiter he had observed taking trays of drinks into the private rooms.

Fortunately, Colin's own drink was instantly recognisable. Because of his attitude to fitness it was non-alcoholic, mainly high in vitamins from the fruit cocktail which comprised the race ground's speciality for teetotallers, a Musselborough Sling. He took the waiter aside just as he was approaching the door, and said, 'A quiet word, quickly please.' The guy was about to refuse, when he saw the three £20 notes David was offering.

David said, 'All I want you to do, is to see if, whilst serving the drinks, you hear any particular horses being mentioned as potential winners. I really would love to increase my chances of making a big score today.' The young man, a student working for some holiday cash agreed but asked that it might be made up to £100. Whilst he was putting the money away, he did not notice David tipping the bottle of knock out drugs into the Musselborough Sling.

David drove the ambulance around to the rear of the club where he knew there was a private entrance to Derek's, now Colin's suite. Sure enough, after about ten minutes he heard the call for an ambulance. He waited another five then drove round the corner and parked immediately in front of the door with emergency lights flashing and siren sounding. One of the many things he had learnt was that his victim very well guarded by Cafferty and two strong men from the gang called Sandy and Tim. They certainly looked the part, both with big, muscled bodies as they carried their unconscious leader out to the ambulance.

This time Cafferty and Tim insisted on going with him but agreed when David said, 'Sorry guys, I'm even bending the rules to let one of you come but there is, just not the room for me to do my work if there are two. Why don't one of you come and the others can follow us on by car to the hospital. You can be with your boss there, if that's okay with them. They agreed and Tim got in and sat on the bed opposite Colin. David asked Tim to keep a close eye on the flashing BP monitor he had attached to his patient, then headed away.

It was time for repetition. David pulled into a quiet back passageway behind a block of offices now closed for the weekend. He stunned and drugged Tim. then heaved him out and left him propped up against a wall.

After this David headed off around the city bypass until he connected with the A67 south.

What he did not know was that one of the reasons

Cafferty was so highly regarded was that he had a very suspicious nature. He was always watching out for anything out of the usual which might lead to harm for his boss. This time, while they had been carrying Colin out, he remembered something niggling away at the back of his mind. Did he not hear something about an ambulance in the tale of Mike's recent ordeal in London which was doing the rounds? Better safe than sorry, he thought, and went to get a locating bug from the office safe. As they were securing Colin in the ambulance, he knelt and stuck it to the inside of its rear bumper.

He took Sandy back into the boss's office and turned on the laptop. The ambulance showed up as a blinking red light. It travelled away, then stopped for a short while, then it set off again. He assumed the driver had just been checking up on his patient, but when it drove on, it was not heading anywhere near the direction to the hospital. He watched grimly as it turned south down the A68 towards Melrose. He waited until it had stopped for some time and carefully noted the co-ords and marked them on his road map. Then Cafferty got Sandy and another gangster into his car and off towards where the ambulance had gone. They were about one hour down the road when they got a phone call from Tim, He had recovered sufficiently to tell Cafferty all that had happened.

Arriving at the farmhouse, David secured the wheelchair to the bolts in the floor of the cabinet in the bathroom. He gave his prisoner another injection, thinking he needed to be careful not to overdo it. David left the house, got onto his motorbike and drove back to where the farm access track met the main road. He took a camcorder out of his knapsack and secured it in bushes at the side of the road overlooking the entrance and turned it on. It was well hidden. Then he biked back down to just where the farm road lead to the open area before the entrance to the house. He concealed another camcorder behind a tree overlooking the road the track. Back in the house he fastened a gag to Colin's mouth, fixed on his mask then opened the cold water tap to let a dribble feed out towards his captive.

Now he went into the lounge and turned on the cameras which were linked to his laptop. He checked both alarms were working. After a well-earned cup of tea and some delicious cheese scones he had purchased, it was time for a rest. David drifted into a deep sleep. About three hours later he was wakened by the incessant buzz coming from the computer screen. The alarm by the access to the farm road had been triggered. He carefully watched as one man he thought Cafferty, who had obviously been waiting, was joined by another two who arrived driving a black Range Rover. They stood outside eating what looked like fish suppers. When they'd finished, they got into the car and drove down the track towards the house. David waited until he saw them again through the lower camera by the entrance. He belted on his revolver, took a stun gun and three of the Tasers and lay down in the hallway, concealed behind a coat stand. He aimed a Taser at the front door.

The men pulled up quietly by the entrance and took out their pistols. David heard two sets of footsteps coming up to the front door. Another set went round to the rear as you would have expected. There was a very loud crash as two sledgehammers crashed through the locked front door. The two men came in waving guns and yelling out, 'Right, you bastard, you're surrounded, we've got guns, come out!'

David Tasered first Cafferty and then took another to Sandy, the man with him. He ran over to them, gave them each a dose of drugs to keep them still. Then, grabbing his last Taser he turned to his concealed position to watch over the kitchen door. He heard the tinkle of breaking glass, then heard footsteps as the third man opened the door and came out into the hallway. He soon was lying flat out on the floor with his mates. David injected him and tied him up in the same way as the others.

By this time Colin was coming blearily awake. What the hell was this, tied to a chair in a shower cabinet, and what was that rammy outside? The cabinet door and the door of the room had been left open so he could see clearly into the hall. There Cafferty, Sandy and Matt lay unconscious on the floor tied up. He heard his captor's voice behind him.

'Right, Colin, perhaps this will bring you to your senses or at least the little sense you possess. This is what happens when you try and mess with me. People have tried before to tangle with me and have met an even worse fate than your henchmen. They have been very lucky in that all I've done so far is knock them out and drugged them heavily. I will give them another injection before we leave. But in the meantime, just you sit here looking at them and thinking very carefully through how you are going to react to my demands.'

David then went into the lounge and poured a cup of coffee. He sat in his comfortable chair reflecting on what had happened. Aileen had told him that the minimum time, even a big man would be knocked out by the drug would be roughly over an hour, so he had plenty of time to think through what it was that had gone wrong, and what he should do about it. Clearly this was the end of the Borders hideout. From now on he could either use Derby or look for another base, probably in mid Scotland.

Also, it was almost certain that the ambulance had been identified, perhaps by locating devices. He decided to take it with Colin to his base in Derby and then leave it there. From now on he would use the builders' van. Next, how the hell did they track him down? He thought through everything he'd done, all his movements to date. He knew his telephone could not have been tapped, he knew it was unlikely he had been observed, as he followed Colin on his routines, so the likelihood was that a bug locator had been attached, probably to the ambulance at the race course. David took out the scanning wand which he'd purchased in Currys at the same time as his computer. He carefully went over the vehicle inch by inch. He only found one. It was hidden behind the rear bumper.

However, when he looked at the scanner again, he saw there was still a flashing warning light. He went over the ambulance once more. There was nothing. So the likelihood was that having learned of his exploits elsewhere, the criminals had thought it would be a good idea to hide a tracing bug on their boss. Either in his clothes or on his body. David carefully scanned all the clothes he'd taken off, there was nothing. So, starting at his feet he scanned Colin's naked body. It bleeped as it got to the middle of his left thigh. Where, looking carefully, he could see a neatly stitched up incision. Taking a sharp knife from the cutlery drawer David sliced it open and fished in the wound. He located the small device and pulled it out. Going into the garage he smashed the two bugs with a large hammer. The scan now showed nothing. No alarms.

David was now sure that everything was safe for him to leave. He went into the hallway to give the three criminals a further injection, and then stabbed the syringe into Colin's shoulder. It only took five or so minutes before he started to collapse. Again, using the same knife, he cauterised the wound in Colin's thigh. David went over to the gang's Range Rover and sliced open all four tyres. The knockout drug should keep them still for a while, but there was no harm in adding belts to braces.

David again put Colin into the ambulance, drove him along the track out onto the road, and through the small country roads towards the English border. He stopped in a garage by a large Morrisons supermarket just on the northern outskirts of Berwick. There he dialled 999, and when a female voice replied said, 'Listen carefully please. The police need to go into Megget Manor. It is west of Melrose and just to the west of the village of Capperhaugh. Inside the manor house they will find three gangsters. I have drugged them unconscious as they came armed with guns to rob me.' The female constable said 'Thank you sir, could I have your name and—' The call terminated. David threw that mobile phone over a hedge into some rough grassland, got back into the ambulance and headed off south towards the A19 and his route back to Derby.

David pushed the wheelchair with an unconscious Colin, who once again had been drugged, into the shower cabinet and secured the chair to the floor. He drove the ambulance into the garage beside the van and motorbike and securely locked the door. He then used the zip ties to tightly fasten the wheels of the chair to the bolts he'd drilled into the bathroom floor, then went to bed for a well-earned sleep.

The next morning, he was woken from a deep sleep by muffled swearing from the bathroom. He went in and stood behind Colin pointing the stun gun down the back of his neck as the insults grew viler.

So David gave him a quick burst with the stun gun, then, as he struggled back awake tapped the rear of Colin's head hard with a wooden post he'd left there.

He said right, 'If you think your swearing and threats are going to make an inch of difference you are sadly mistaken. Nobody knows where you are, and you don't have a clue where you are, nor who I am.

'You have read the list of demands for information and the funds I intend to get from you. You may still be thinking that your gang will try once again to locate you. I should let you know that I have found and destroyed the locating bugs in the ambulance and also removed the one inserted into your left thigh. You should be able to feel a slight pain, and if you look down at your leg you will see the bandage covering the scar I made removing it. So you have no chance of getting any help. Furthermore, you should be aware by now from the rumours you've heard and from what you've seen so far, I have successfully kidnapped you from your gang HQ. I have travelled a long way with you safely secured. I have disabled not only your gang but your vicious bodyguard, Cafferty. I promise you, I can do a lot worse.

'I don't give a hoot about you and what happens to you. I don't care how much pain, distress and suffering you have to experience. It will be nothing compared to the damage and suffering you have caused to so many people's lives. I intend to keep you here, secured in this wheelchair for up to three days. You will be fed basic food and water. If, by the end of that time, you have not agreed to my demands, I will start torturing you extremely painfully. I will start by fastening an electrode from the mains to your balls. It won't take long before you will dislike the burning smell as they are burnt to ashes.

'I have drugs and various tools and can cause you a huge amount of extreme pain. If, however, you manage to get through all of that, then I will end my campaign and kill you. We are in a very isolated part of our country but within half a mile or so, is a large working farm. They are known for the very successful piggery they run. The pigs will eat almost anything but prefer flesh. I will not kill you but slice open your body so you're bleeding all over the place, and tip you over the wall of the pigsty, late at night. You will have vanished completely by the morning, bones and all.'

It did not take three days, just two. Colin said he was prepared to give the information that David wanted, as well as the money. The following morning David set up his recording equipment including the camera, and filmed as Colin spilled all the info he could about his drugs trade; his dealers; what drugs were available how he got hold of them; and when and where. He also gave David a full description of each of the main members of his gang, together with the crimes they had committed. The next day, Colin sat in the chair cursing. He'd given up everything he knew, trade, partners and drugs. Where this would lead to, particularly if the information was passed to the police, he dreaded to think.

That night David again drugged Colin and took him secured into the wheelchair into the back of the builder's van. He fixed the chair to the bolts he had drilled into the metal floor. It took him about three and a half hours to drive from Derby back to Edinburgh. He intended to arrive at his destination at 3 a.m. when the place should be very still and there would be little risk of him being observed. He pulled up just beside a bus shelter along the road which led to Murrayfield, Scotland's main rugby stadium.

Looking carefully all around to check he was not being

watched, he opened the van doors, took out the wheelchair and pushed it into the shelter. He snipped through all the wires securing his prisoner, then dragged Colin out and propped him up against one of the seats. He gave him a final injection to keep him unconscious until he would be discovered by an alarmed bus passenger early the next morning.

David then drove south heading for the A1 and back to his Derby base. It was time to meet up again with Roberta.

# Chapter 11

# Roberta

Roberta was quite pleased with herself. By working hard during the day and in the evenings she had significantly reduced the massive backlog of work facing her.

Now it was time to research Alan Carter. She had been in no doubt that it was a fake name, as fake as the ginger hairpiece, moustache and little beard he had adopted. It certainly never occurred to her that he also might be enhancing his height.

She went in to see her boss, Nigel, early the next morning.

'Nigel, can I have a word please.'

'Roberta, you know you're my favourite writer, just fire away.' She explained in outline her involvement with Alan, his sad family tale and that he had promised a series of headline grabbing articles later on in the year.

'Sounds fascinating, Roberta, but we're hell of a busy just now, so what is it you want?'

'I want time off so that I can really carefully research the true facts behind this man and his campaign of vengeance. I would like to track down who he really is, where he comes from, and dig deeply into the sad story of his family tragedy. I therefore would need at least two weeks off work to concentrate only on this.'

'Sorry Roberta, no can do. Things are going to get even more hectic here as we approach the general election. You are our most valuable political writer for the newspaper. I'm sorry, I cannot agree to you having time off work.'

'Nigel, I somehow thought that might be your answer, so here's my letter of resignation which takes effect this Friday.'

No matter how Nigel tried, nothing could persuade her to change her mind. He therefore felt he had no option but to grant her a fortnight's unpaid leave. His only condition was that she would start work on the story about Alan and submit regular reports to him.

Roberta sat at her desk making careful notes of the few facts that she had. She was pretty sure that Alan was a Scotsman and probably lived and worked in the Highlands. Also, that not long ago, a young girl had lost her life, almost certainly due to drugs. She was probably a student between seventeen and twenty-three years old. Then, round about the same period, her mother took her own life.

Roberta's letter to the police forces in Glasgow, Edinburgh, Aberdeen, Inverness and Dumfries, resulted in only one real clue which pointed her to Inverness, the capital of the Scottish Highlands. Then a careful trawl through the register of births, deaths and marriages ended the first part of her hunt. Eilidh Mackay aged twenty died in a student flat the previous November. Then, just ten months ago, her mother Helen, was found by her husband, David, having hung herself in the family home in a place called Poolewe in Wester Ross.

'So, David Mackay, at long last we meet.'

The next week, Roberta flew from London to Inverness. As the plane descended for landing she gazed out of the window at splendid scenery. Well maintained farm fields led inland to a series of dramatic mountain peaks. She took the bus from the airport into the centre of the town where she had booked into a convenient B&B. The next day she had a fine Scottish breakfast then she telephoned Inverness police and eventually spoke to DS Stuart McKenzie.

He agreed to meet her for lunch in his favourite Indian restaurant called Sams in the centre of town. After the waiter served them their Cobra lagers and starters, Stuart said, 'Right, Roberta, start at the beginning of your contact with David Mackay. Tell me all you know about him. I want to know why you are researching Eilidh's suicide. I ask in particular because, of all the unpleasant issues I've had to deal with in my career as a policeman, that one affected me deeply. She was so young, I heard she was very clever, and she was certainly attractive. Eilidh seemed to have everything going for her.'

Roberta gave a brief account of her first contact with David and her increasing involvement in the story about his family. However, she did not want to give away too much to this sharp, clever policeman.

'Well, well, so he's going after the thugs who set up these county line gangs. I do detest them probably almost as much as Mr Mackay, but of course as you would understand I am constrained to strictly observe the law when trying to deal with them. Your man David is free of such problems and I wish him all the very best with whatever happens.'

It was late in the afternoon when they left. Stuart said, 'Thank you for such a pleasant meal, it was very good to meet you and I wish you so well with your research. I shall thoroughly look forward to reading all about what's been going on in your newspaper.'

Roberta made an appointment with Ann Davies who she had learned had been David's PA and secretary for many years. She was delighted to hear that Roberta had met him in London and when she said he looked very well. Ann told the reporter all about the formation of David's company, how it was one of the first in the Highlands to see the advance of green energy.

Also, how they had built trial generating plants using wind, air and tidal, funded mainly with government grants to carry out such research.

She said that David had been the man leading and promoting the work, that he was very popular and was asked to speak at environmental conferences all across the world. It was clear that she held her boss in great esteem, maybe personally a lot more!

Roberta then visited what been Eilidh's student flat but the new owners wanted nothing to do with her, they had no wish to be reminded of what had happened. She then met Brodie, Eilidh's ex-boyfriend who told her how her early death had shocked and horrified all of her friends. Roberta's last mission was to Poolewe to look into Eilidh's home life.

Roberta travelled to David's home, which was now rented by new people. But from the Mackay's neighbours she got a lot of information about how he and his wife had been friendly, courteous and always ready to help. They said how sad they been about the tragic deaths of the youngest daughter and then her mother.

Collecting a bouquet of wildflowers, rhododendrons, meadowsweet and tufted vetch, Roberta then made her way into the small graveyard behind the village. She placed her bouquet by the gravestone which showed Eilidh and Helen's names. Roberta stood for a while thinking respectfully, and prayed that David's campaign would help him deal with these terrible events and perhaps look forward to a new life.

Well satisfied with the results of her research, Roberta sat on the plane looking at the photograph Ann, the secretary, had given her of David and his wife in evening dress. They were entering the ballroom where the company's annual Christmas celebration was being held. He certainly was a fine-looking man, with that thought she dozed off.

# Chapter 12

# Newcastle

The Geordie capital of Newcastle upon Tyne was next on the list for a visit from David. He had spent some time there on business but did not in any way pretend he knew the area or its people well. His next target was known as Big Malc.

However, David was now forced, as he suspected might happen, to radically change his plans. It was clear that the ambulance had now been identified by criminals, maybe also the police. So it would now have to stay, locked up in Derby. Also, his hideout in the Borders had been found so he decided to make use again of Derby for his next victim, then find somewhere further north for Glasgow.

Malcolm Wilson was born to Geordie parents who lived in Durham Street, Wallsend. His father, Archie, was a welder in the nearby Swan Hunter's shipyard. His mother, Rachel, had been delighted at his successful birth but very disappointed to learn from the doctor that she would not be able to have any more than her one child. She decided to be a loving wife, housekeeper and mother until Malc was a bit older and his dad could look after him while she again sought a job. Rachel had previously been an air hostess with Easyjet. So she had been used to quite a glamourous existence in exotic places, often being pursued by handsome pilots. Archie had met her at the Palais dance floor in central Newcastle. He was absolutely astounded when this amazing beauty agreed to go out with him, and even more so when, later on, she agreed to be his wife. Archie worked long hours at the shipyard and, like most of his mates on the way home, would call in at the Wallsend working man's club for a few beers and chat.

Malc grew up to be something of a tearaway, a bit of a wild boy. He kept getting into scraps at school and soon found he was quite good at fighting. The only boy who had ever beaten him was called Eddie Gordon who happened to be bigger and stronger than Malc. At this time, it was Eddie who got him involved in his own criminal world, the local gang in Wallsend. They were always looking for youngsters to act as runners to carry messages between hardened criminals and at times even drugs and packets of weapons to their various contacts.

As Malc grew, he became more involved with Eddie and the two of them decided to start their own gang. In the early days, apart from a little pickpocketing, their main activity was nicking from shops. One would distract the shopkeeper's attention by yelling out something while the other would stick a packet of sweets, an item of clothing, or a book inside their jacket and make their way out of the store.

There were a number of young gangs in the area. It soon became necessary to make their mark with them. Eddie and Malc were soon closely united and became friends, particularly when in one battle with a gang from North Shields, someone tripped Eddie up and Malc flattened the lad just as he was about to kick Eddie in the head as he lay helpless. Soon the criminal underworld were using all of their gang to help with business. When he was about fourteen, Malc became really involved in the drugs scene. It was Eddie who got hold of some cannabis and tried to get him to smoke the sweet-smelling drug. Malc was sick at first, then grew to quite like it. However, he had seen plenty of real addicts as he'd gone about the business and had absolutely no intention of heading down that road

The big change came when, with information from one of the gangsters, they learnt that a Newcastle gang was due to collect a consignment of mixed drugs from a ship anchored in the docks just to the east of the town centre. The other gang's plan was to take the drugs back to a disused factory that they often used as their base and share some of the drugs out between them. The majority would go to one of the other gangsters. Malc, Eddie and five of their gang waited inside the factory. The other youngsters had no sooner arrived when they jumped out, grabbed them, then, holding knives to their throats, took their drugs. They quickly made their way off in a stolen van.

However, what did not know was that the police had been aware of this drugs shipment and were watching the Newcastle gang's activities. Eddie and Malc collected their haul and then went out of the factory. As the van drove away and down Jarrow Road they were suddenly boxed in by three squad cars with flashing lights and sirens wailing. Armed police leapt out of the cars, surrounded them, and yelled at them to come out, hands up.

Malc was only sixteen but was sentenced in the juvenile court to 12 months in a Young Offenders Institution. In prison he agreed of course to take counselling to avoid a heavier sentence although in reality he had no intention of taking any notice of it.

Meanwhile back home, both Rachel and Archie had been horrified, first of all to learn of their son's involvement with drugs and then that he'd been arrested by the police and jailed. One of Archie's closest friends was Tom Dixon, in fact they had met at school. Tom was a senior detective sergeant with Newcastle CID. Archie asked Tom to join him for a quiet session in the member's room of the Wallsend club. Archie began to tell Tom what had happened to his son, but Tom interrupted him, and said, 'Archie, I know all about it. It was my squad who were involved in entrapping the gang who received these drugs and I of course am aware of what happened to your son and his gang and of the sentence that he has received to spend 12 months in prison. What is it you want of me?'

'I honestly don't know, Tom, you are my closest friend and of course I would not ask you to do anything that would in any way risk or damage your career but if there is anything at all you could do to help mitigate this sentence, maybe get it reduced, we would both be deeply grateful. But if it is more sensible that my idiot of a son serves his time and learns a painful lesson, please just say. I will then speak to him directly and ram the lesson he should have learnt, though I doubt it, down his throat so that he never goes anywhere near the drugs trade again.'

'Archie, I am pretty sure I can't do anything about the sentence, but I certainly will have a long chat with your son myself. I was thinking of doing that anyway; he is far too young to be starting down a criminal road.'

Malc had taken full advantage of the gym exercise equipment in the prison. After six months of regular, at times extreme, exercise, his body began to fill out and he was having a growing sprint anyway. So Eddie and some of his other mates began to call him Big Malc. One month before the end of his sentence, Malc was surprised to receive a summons to the governor's office. When he went in he was astonished to see not only the governor but DS Tom Dixon, his father's best mate dressed in his police uniform. DS Dixon ran through several tales about youngsters who become involved in the drug scene and how they came to, at times, sticky and rather horrible ends. He repeated over and over again that somebody in Malc's position, with loving and caring parents and a decent home, should not be in such trouble. That he should be looking for another way of passing his time as a youth rather than it being in crime.

By now, Rachel had done as she had planned. She felt that re-joining the tourist air-travel companies would mean far too many trips away, so she applied for a job as a tour guide with a new company called Riviera Travel. Most of their holidays were in Europe, catering mainly for Brits. With her previous training, good looks and natural intelligence, Rachel was soon a highly regarded member of Riviera's staff. In a couple of years she was promoted to be a senior cruise leader and then on to become a cruise director for Portugal and Spain. The week before Big Malc was due to be released, she asked to see her boss for a private session. She told him what had happened to her son, about his life and of the opportunities that he could have had. She described him as good-looking, that he was very popular with people he met, and was very quick on the uptake. She suggested that he would make an excellent tourist guide with their holiday company.

'Okay Rachel, you been such a success with the company, I think we will agree to grant you this request, on one condition. You make it clear, in no uncertain terms to your son that, if he has any involvement whatsoever with drugs or crime, he will be out of the job so quickly, we won't waste time on paperwork.'

Archie went to pick Malc up at the prison that weekend and drove him home. Rachel made a nice meal.

When they had enjoyed it she said, 'Right, Malc, Archie and I want to speak to you very seriously about your future.' Both made it eminently clear that his time within the drugs scene was at a complete end. They said that he needed to find a new way forward with his life. Rachel then explained what her work was about with the travel company and said, 'They do have a junior position. Riviera are prepared to give you a try, will you have a go, my son?'

It didn't take long for Malc to see how he had been wasting his time. The reality was that he had been getting fed up with the activities of his onetime friends and the criminals they encountered.

Malc was appointed as a junior tour guide working alongside a senior who was teaching him the trade. They would meet tourists coming off planes in France, get them into a coach, then give them a week's touring of the French countryside in whatever region they had chosen. Malc had done some French in school and had a schoolboy's knowledge but was determined to improve himself. So he took French language lessons and after just over a year was able to communicate, albeit with a strong Geordie accent, with the French people he met. Just like his mother Rachel, he did extremely well and was soon thought of as one of their potential stars. He was given the position of tour guide in charge of all the arrangements himself and successfully carried that out for about five years. Next the company asked him to take on the position of senior guide on their cruise ship on the river Douro in northern Portugal.

Again, Malc became highly regarded and in fact people asking for return holidays would often question if he could be booked as their guide. But the company were doing very well in having him employed in Portugal, particularly as he was now trying to learn the Portuguese language. The cruise in northern Portugal was one of the company's most popular offerings.

What nobody knew back in the company's offices was that one of the catering staff on board the vessel had arranged a wild night out in the ancient city of Porto for the staff. Big Malc was hugely enjoying the nonsense when one of his new friends, a Portuguese lad called Vadik, offered him a joint. He had no sooner started to like it when he was given another. It did not take long before Big Malc again became hooked. It also wasn't long before some of the tourists who were interested, learnt that he could obtain drugs for them. This probably would been accepted as unpleasant but permissible until he started offering to supply cocaine and heroin. One of the passengers complained to the cruise director and within that week Malc was on a plane back home.

This time there was no nice meal waiting. Just a furious Rachel and Archie telling him, 'Bugger off, if that's the life you want, go and find it somewhere else. Live elsewhere and do what you want with your life. We want nothing more to do with you, we tried our best.'

Big Malc took his bag and contacted Eddie, who by now was one of the important criminals on Tyneside. He was delighted to have his old friend back and soon gave him a senior position with the gang, as well as a room in the large flat he was renting. By this time the drug scene was the number one activity for the gangs in Newcastle. Constantly imports of all kind of drugs were being successfully sneaked ashore at the docks and jetties up and down the River Tyne. Also, they started using youngsters in the outlying districts like Morpeth, Hexham, South Shields and Durham to form their own junior gangs and deal with drugs themselves, thereby distancing the trade from Eddie and Malc.

It was about ten years after this that Eddie fell very ill with cancer. This left him weak and very unfit to continue the business. He thus handed it all over to Big Malc. Now Malc's reputation grew and grew and soon he was not only highly regarded in the north-east of England but had established contacts in the drugs trade in some of England's other main cities.

David learnt that Big Malc, who was now nearing sixty years old, was living in a very expensive, detached villa in Darras Hall, one of the most expensive and exclusive districts of Newcastle. David by now was becoming concerned that information about his previous captures might have resulted in them being talked about by gangsters all over the place, including Newcastle. Therefore, he decided against trying to rent a house in this exclusive area, when he could easily keep an eye on Big Malc by drone. So instead, David rented a student flat, in nearby Ponteland. Every day he would set off and park his car in a secluded layby. There he would fly his drone above the avenue which led from Big Malc's luxurious home. As he began to learn all about his target's routine, he had one drone fly around 9 a.m., a second at 7 p.m., and the third at 9 p.m. to find out what he was up to. It only took about eight days before he discovered how Malc was retaining his personal links with the leading members of his gangs.

Malc, was using his old haunt, Wallsend working man's club. Every Tuesday night, a taxi would collect him at 7.30 and take him to the club. Then he would be picked up from the club at 9.30 to be returned home.

David waited in his car watching these comings and goings. The taxi driver was almost always the same man. Malc must have asked for him. The driver would return at 9.15, leaving quarter of an hour before the time planned for picking him up. David intended to use that fifteen minutes well. The taxi pulled into a side lane to wait there for Malc. David went up to the waiting driver and knocked on his window. When it opened and the driver asked what he wanted, David stunned him, then injected him with the syringe. Next, he heaved him out of the driver's door and using his ankle and wrist cuffs bundled him into a squatting position by a garage, unconscious.

David returned to the cab and waited. Almost on the dot of 9.30, Malc came out, walked over looking surprised and said 'Where's Pete?' David said.

'He's been taken ill with some kind of tummy bug. The boss asked me to come and pick you up.' So Malc got into the back without suspecting anything wrong. He was further surprised when the driver slid open the glass partition between them, pointed the stun gun at him and knocked him back into the seat. After similarly securing him with the zip ties David gave him an injection from another syringe, knocking him out completely. David drove the taxi down to the commercial area just by the side of Swan Hunters and into a lane of mainly disused businesses. He went to the double garage he had rented for the month, opened the door and transferred Big Malc into the wheelchair secured within the workman's van. He then drove the van away heading towards the A19 and his route south to Derby.

But things had not gone at all as he had planned. An old lady living in her council flat opposite the lane where the taxi halted had seen what was going on. David getting in to replace the driver after he'd tied him up, then leaving him on the pavement. Then she saw him using what looked like a gun on the passenger. Next, he dragged the passenger out and into a builder's van parked back up the lane. She phoned the police and in her quavering voice recounted what she seen. Fortunately, Detective Chief Inspector Ridley was on duty and took the transferred call. He had been the one keeping up to date with the interesting tales from elsewhere in England, of attacks on drugs barons. This sounded very much like another one. Could it really be one of these? He knew of course of Big Malc's reputation and about his regular meetings with his crew. So DCI Ridley phoned the working man's club and asked to speak to Mr Malcolm Wilson. A rather panicky, mumbling voice said 'Sorry, can't talk just now. I am afraid Mr Wilson has left the premises.'

That was enough, he called the troops together and set up a major incident enquiry. He demanded that roadblocks be set up on the six main routes exiting the city and gave each one a description of the builder's van and its number plate. After nearly half an hour at the road block on the A19 just south of Seaton, PC Brian Syms and policewoman Hazel Dixon saw a builder's van come towards them, moving fast but steadily. PC Syms stepped out to the centre of the road and waved his hand for it to stop.

'Here it comes, get ready, Hazel,' he yelled as he saw the van travelling towards them. It had the correct markings. It screeched to a halt a short distance away from their ambush. A man wearing overalls got out of the driver's seat. Brian used the bullhorn to boom out, 'Armed police, lie down on the ground with your arms stretched out in front of you.'

The driver did no such thing. He had a Taser gun in each hand. He first knocked out PC Syms then fired the other at Hazel. They both fell down flat. David went across and heaved each of them into a more comfortable position. Then he zip tied them and gave both an injection of drugs. He took the keys out of the ignition of the police car and threw them over a hedge. Bloody hell, that was far too close. The coppers were onto me fast, how the hell did they know what I was up to?

With Big Malc safely secured, David sat in the lounge nursing a very large tumbler of malt whisky. The only thing he could think of was that someone had spotted his kidnap and phoned the police. He considered looking for another vehicle but that really was too much. He was at the stage of being increasingly tired. He had nearly had enough, so decided he would risk using the van for the final occasion. He would though take it into Derby to have it completely re-sprayed and re-badged, this time as electrical repair company.

We don't know whether it was Big Malc's supreme level of fitness but the drugs seem to wear off him more quickly than it had in some of the other victims. He came to around 2.30 in the morning. Malc sat quietly taking in his situation and his surroundings. He tried twisting his arms and legs but he was too tightly secured. However, one thing David did not know, was that when Big Malc was young, just a little lad, he'd been very interested in tales of escapologists like the great Houdini who he'd actually seen in a carnival on Newcastle's Town Moor. He'd read a couple of books about similar people. He learnt that, using a combination of physical and mental strengths, what they would do was to concentrate extremely hard and make their ankles and wrists swell before bindings were attached. So that later they would allow their limbs to relax and with great strength, be able to twist themselves free. Big Malc decided to do the same. He sat until dawn, contemplating what he would do to this swine when he eventually got free. Around 7 a.m. David came into the shower room and turned it on full. Although Malc gasped he gave no other outward sign. He sat quietly, listening as David presented his list of demands and told him in no uncertain terms what was going to happen to him Then Malc asked permission to speak. David was taken aback. This was a new one. 'What do you want?'

'As you may know I have kept myself very fit throughout my life. You can see that from my body. Therefore, I am finding these ties extremely restrictive. Is there any chance that you could release them, stand at the back of the room, and keep your gun pointed at me, but at least allow me to stroll around the area in front of the chair and loosen my limbs and muscles before I start to have blood problems.'

David couldn't see any reason to object so snipped the ties and moved near the door pointing his revolver and a Taser at Big Malc. Malc stiffly stood up and hobbled round and round in a small circle in front of the wheelchair. He then sat down again and said 'Thank you, you can tie me up again.' David did so, administered another dose of drugs after an electric shock and went out. He got into the van and drove off towards the garage he had phoned who were ready to do a quick respray.

Big Malc now let his limbs relax and using his great strength, forced a wrist free. Then he reached down and pulled away the ties holding his ankles. Stiffly, he rose and went over to where David had dumped his clothes in a corner. He dressed and had a quick prowl around the place. Malc found, as he had expected that it was empty, so made his way out and onto the farm access road. He could see a town on a hill not far from him. He started to walk along the road. A workman's van came towards him from the direction of the town. Big Malc waved and waved as if in a panic. The van stopped and Malc reeled back in horror, as a familiar-looking figure stepped out onto the road

Unluckily for Big Malc, David's cautious nature had triggered a worry as he drove off towards the garage. He realised that he hadn't set alarms in the house, nor in the drive and was returning back to do just that when he spotted his captive hobbling along. Now he took Big Malc back into his chair and secured his legs and arms extremely tightly with two pairs of zip ties for each limb. When Big Malc came to, David entered and said, 'Well, I have to congratulate you, my first victim to have found his way out of my prison chair. It was pure luck that I happened to be returning and got you. But now there is no escape. Not only have I doubled up on the ties securing you but I have installed movement alarms by the door of this room and the door of the house. Should you by some freak trick be able to get out again they will trigger alerts to me and then you will suffer very painfully. Do you understand, Big Malc?'

By now Big Malc was starting to appreciate just what a difficult position he was in. He looked up at the sheet of paper pinned in front of him with the list of demands. He said to David, 'I tell you what, I'm prepared to go along with some of your demands. You can have the money, I'll talk about my gangs, and I'll tell you some of the people that I sell the drugs to. But I will not tell you about those that I buy them from, nor about the various gangs we sell to. Do you accept that?'

David said, 'No, I insist on all my demands, but it was worth a try. I am now going to give you another electric shock then a dose of drugs. When you come to you will have the same again. That will last for at least three days until you break down as all my prisoners have before. Do you understand?'

Malc said yes. On day two, having thought things through very carefully, Big Malc spilled the beans.

# Chapter 13

## Glasgow

At last, this was the end of a long, lonely, hectic year. David was very pleased with his success to date. He felt that he had done significant damage to the criminal trade in drugs. But what a great location to end with. Glasgow had always been one of his favourite cities. This large, tough, self-confident industrial place was where he had met more Scotsmen he had respected than anywhere else. He loved the Glaswegian's non-stop patter and the way they always made fun of themselves but heaven help anyone else who tries the same!

Here, the man Roberta had identified was Sean O'Casey, unsurprisingly originally an Irishman. Sean had been brought up in Belfast, another hard city. As he grew up he became more and more involved with the terrorist origination his father Liam belonged to, the Provisional IRA.

Sean O'Casey was born into a Catholic family in 1967 in Belfast. This was just two years before the PIRA (Provisional Irish Republican Army) formed. His father, Liam, had been actively engaged in the armed struggle up until that time. He'd been trained as one of the embryo movement's bomb experts. This gave him a very clear focus on his life. Just give him a few sticks of dynamite and a digital watch and then wait for the bang.

(He could not have been that good however, as he was killed by one of his own explosive devices when Sean was twenty-two years old.)

His address in Belfast was just three streets away from the infamous Falls Road, a flash point for so much of the troubles. Sean was Liam and his wife's seventh child and not the last. It was still fashionable for Catholics in Ireland to create large families. As Sean grew up, he became increasingly aware of his father's involvement with terrorism. Liam was a well-known member of the Provos, the Provisional Irish army, and a proud Irish Roman Catholic, as were almost as all of his mates. He was well known to the British and Irish soldiers and there was a reward for anyone who captured him in action.

His mother Teagan was not at all keen to see another of her brood involved with the IRA activities but Liam had no doubt at all. 'It is every young man's duty to be part of our struggle to gain our freedom,' was his motto.

The worst period of IRA attacks was between 1975 and 1982. During these seven years Sean grew from a lad into a very active teenager. At that time the violence was at its height. In Belfast alone at least twenty-three people were killed, mostly due to sectarian attacks. Most of the PIRA to be caught were taken since 1979. But, convicted Ulster Protestants made up 43% of the prison population. At that time, Catholics were often the victims of savage beatings including threats backed with the use of butcher's knives. One of the worst of the Proddy gangs was in fact known as the Shankill butchers, a Protestant gang with a terrible reputation led by a convicted criminal, Leroy Murphy.

By that time Sean was becoming heavily involved with the IRA. He had started by being one of the kids who would be regularly done for throwing bricks and bottles at the lines of British soldiers and Irish policeman trying to constrain them. No doubt his life would have continued like that if he hadn't been a keenly observant, if not nosy young lad. The PIRA had a local HQ in a street just around the corner from his home. Sean often would lurk around there watching all the comings and goings, in particular whether they were carrying guns – a major thrill.

One evening he was there when he noticed a man making his way into the back of a flat diagonally opposite the HQ. The man was scruffy, wearing tatty denims, and had long, shaggy hair. But it was his bearing that made Sean suspicious. He was erect, almost as if he had a soldiery bearing. Sean followed him in and hid behind some shrubbery at the rear of the house. He saw the man look around very carefully, then open the back door.

After a wee while, Sean followed him in. From the kitchen, he could just hear muffled voices from above. He took off his shoes and very quietly tiptoed up the stairs, He looked into a bedroom where an attic hatch was dangling down. Now he could clearly hear British voices. Bloody hell, this had to be a spy post. They were watching and listening to the men in the house across the road. No doubt noting down who they were and all the comings and goings.

He made his way out, then went over garden walls until he came to the end of the row, He had to be careful in case the bloody Brits spotted him. Sean crossed the road and ran to the rear of the HQ. He hammered on the door to be greeted with a roar of 'What the fuck's that racket?' then, 'What the fuck do you want?'

The commander rapidly changed his tune when he heard what Sean had to tell him. 'Bloody hell, young O'Casey, you've done a smashing job for us. Wait till Liam hears of this, he'll be dead proud. Now bugger off while I get the troops together and we decide what to do.'

Two nights later Sean was getting another real telling off from Liam, for not giving him the news first, when the doorbell rang. The commander came in and once more congratulated Sean. 'Well done, young Sean, you couldn't have timed it better. Those bastards were just about to raid us in force and close us down. We'll be finding a role for you after that.' It was two days later when Liam showed him the *Belfast News*. The bodies of three British soldiers had been found on a farm near the border. They had been severely tortured.

Then, after his news which led to the destruction of the spy post and the soldiers' murders, Sean was encouraged by the local boss to try to learn the bomb trade from his father, Liam. Sean was seventeen, when there was a crash as the door to his home was smashed open and anti-terrorist forces pushed their way in. An informant had given his name and contact details to the Irish army and identified him as an up-and-coming teenage terrorist. This was just a bit too much. Sean escaped through his bedroom window and ran away but later Liam persuaded his son to flee his home country and go to work with his own brother, Terry, who ran a small criminal outfit in Northern England, based in Liverpool.

Sean's uncle Terry had been in England for most of his life and was a well-known criminal in Liverpool. Terry was only too pleased to give his nephew a job as he had heard from his contacts in Ireland just how well the young man had done. Soon Sean was regarded as another up-and-coming gangster. But Sean's ambition extended way beyond that of his uncle. He quite quickly made good contacts with the leaders of the drugs underworld in Glasgow, a huge and growing trade. It took Sean almost no time to become very heavily involved in Scotland's industrial capital. Not before long he was the undisputed 'Heid Man' as the Glaswegians said.

Sean had also contacted a man he'd been in school with, Frank Magee. He had also been a fighter with the Provos. Frank, now the violence was over, was bored and leapt at the opportunity to become Sean's right-hand man and be his personal bodyguard.

After about four months, as his campaign progressed, David received an unexpected message from Roberta. He had retained one mobile phone for the exclusive use of Roberta and his family. Only they knew the telephone number. Roberta said to him, that Sean O'Casey had suffered a major heart attack whilst out jogging and after two days in intensive care had passed away. Sean's wife Gracie was now said to have taken over the reins as the leading gangster and drugs in Glasgow and surrounding areas. But very little was known at this stage about her plans or ambitions.

David sat, turning over the details from Roberta on the

drugs business in Glasgow. But boy, this was going to be such an unusual capture for him. For the very first time his target was a woman which would make things very different. He read on. Gracie was Sean's recent widow. Sean had risen through the ranks of gangsters when he moved from Liverpool. He had soon headed up a number of the gangs both in Glasgow and on both sides of the Clyde. Sean also had very strong links with his opposite numbers in Edinburgh and Aberdeen. His one empire, ran up to £4 million a year. Now Gracie had only been in charge for two months. But by all accounts, she was being very successful and in fact was thought of as even more capable than her violent ex-husband.

David grinned when he read where she lived. This was a large, expensive, detached villa in Milngavie on the north-west edge of Glasgow. It was a place where well-to-do professionals, business people, doctors, dentists and similar sorts of people chose to live. His smile was that this was so similar to the area of Darras Hall by Newcastle where Big Malc had decided to make his home. He thought, Why did criminals signal their wish to lift themselves above their station in such an obvious way?

For the next two weeks David hired an expensive 4x4 Range Rover. This would fit very well into the traffic travelling around Milngavie. He followed Gracie day after day by car, on foot, and using his drone. He soon gathered a very clear picture of her weekly routine. Like all his other targets she held regular meetings with the main figures in her gangs. However, he decided, that because of the likelihood that information about his previous captures will have leaked out and be known in the underworld, this might be too obvious an approach. Therefore, he looked elsewhere.

David decided to make use of Gracie's regular walks with her dog, a Cairn terrier, called McTavish. She would drive, then stroll round the reservoir in Milngavie which formed the main feed for Glasgow i.e. the city's water works. Wearing his builder's costume and taking the wheelchair he hid in some shrubbery near the most isolated part of her walk. As Gracie passed by, he stunned her from behind then did the same to her snarling wee dog. Carefully he lifted Gracie and secured her in the wheelchair using a blanket to conceal her constraints. Then, using the syringe he gave her an injection of the knockout drug. He tied the little whimpering dog to one of the benches located around the walk. Somebody would find it and take it away.

David pushed Gracie in the chair back to where he'd parked the van. He pushed her inside and secured the chair to the floor. Then he drove out of the works and off onto the road which led to Kilsyth. There he proceeded to the bungalow he had rented. David pushed the wheelchair into the centre of the double garage, closed the door and turned the lights on. He then sat, sipping from his flask of tea. After about an hour Gracie began to move groggily and murmur. So he went over to her and removed the gag and blindfold. Blinking against the fierce light she said,

'Well, well, at long last!' Much to his surprise Gracie did not show any either anger or fear. She went on, 'At last you've come! I wondered how long it would take you to capture me. I heard in detail from Colin what happened to him in Edinburgh, what you did and asked of him. He also told me about some of the others in England.

'Now, you have no reason to threaten me. I am more than ready to meet your demands assuming they are the same as presented to Colin. You see, although I dearly loved and much respected my Sean, I have I never liked his involvement with drugs and on numerous occasions tried to talk him into withdrawing from that trade. So, once I recovered from his funeral, over the last month I started to close down the routes he used. I stopped contact with his dealers two months ago.

'I will have ceased all involvement with the drugs trade, which I understand is your main demand, in another month or so. As to the money, it doesn't seem to fit with the principled character you claim to be, just a victim of this evil trade. What do you want it for?'

‘I intend to use it to fund my campaign so that my remaining family do not suffer any more than they have already. The remainder will go to charities which deal with victims of drug abuse.’

‘Okay, please tell me what drove you to this, what was it that affected you so deeply?’

After she had listened very carefully to the full account of David’s tragic tale, Gracie sat back quietly, moisture forming at the edge of her eyes.

‘What a terrible horrible thing to happen. No wonder you’ve caused such chaos to Sean’s illegal trade. I’ll tell you what though, I will of course say nothing to anyone of what you've done or told me. Also, I have been left very comfortably off, so I will send to you, not two hundred thousand pounds, but half a million pounds.’

David could hardly overcome his shock. At long last he was dealing with a sympathetic and human being.

Just as he started to release Gracie from her constraints she said, ‘Hold on a little. I have just thought of something else that might suit both of us very well. You will of course have learnt about Frank Magee, Sean’s number 2. He’s a very nasty piece of work. I have never come across a more evil, twisted psycho. He tried to have his way with me, the dirty bastard. When I told him where to put his tiny pecker, he told me, that if I breathed a word about it to Sean, he would say that it had been all my doing, that I had told him I really fancied him. So of course, I have said nothing at all. But now’s the time to pay the bastard back.

‘Do you remember the story about the murder of the two kids who had been dealing for the gang? They were only fourteen, but had fallen on bad times and it was rumoured they were going to act as spies for the polis. Their naked bodies, well, what was left of them, were found in the piggery of a farm run by one of Frank’s own mob. Luckily for them they had been killed before their horrible deaths. It was Frank who shot them, and I will write down detailed instructions on where to find the weapon he used and hid. I would bet a hundred quid it will still have the lazy bastard’s fingerprints all over it. The Glasgow polis force have for years tried to catch that thug, now's their chance.'

David rocked back in his chair. This was beyond his wildest dreams. For the first time he took a good look at Gracie. My goodness, Sean certainly knew how to pick them. He had learnt that she was a true Glaswegian but her flashing green eyes and deep reddish hair betrayed her Celtic ancestry. She was not only a looker however, as she had revealed, Gracie was a deep thinker and one determined to do well in the world. He sighed. Maybe if things had turned out a bit differently, he could have found a new romance. But no, he was already spoken for.

David thanked her very much, then drove her home, to where the pair made what was for Gracie, a tearful farewell.

# Chapter 14

## Roberta again

The telephone on her desk rang insistently. Sighing she put down the draft article she had been writing about the growth of county lines, drugs gangs across the country. She intended it to be the opener to the start of her writings about Alan and his campaign. 'Hello, this is Roberta.'

'Good morning Roberta, Alan Carter.'

'Hello Alan, how good to hear from you. How are you, how's your campaign going?'

'That is the reason for the call, Roberta. At last I am finished. I have achieved all I set out to and more with your valuable help.'

'I would like to meet up with you and hand over the information that I have collected for you. There is a hell of a story in it for you, even a likely bestseller. How's about lunch?'

The reporter responded enthusiastically, 'Great, I will change my plans. Do you fancy going to our usual place, Italian cuisine suits me fine. I am already tasting the king prawn linguine.'

When they sat down at the table and ordered food and wine she said 'Well, Alan, it is really great to see you again, even though you are looking tired. I, of course, am aware of some of the things you've been up to from my informers and Internet gossip. You've had a hell of a busy time of it from all accounts it is no wonder you look exhausted. Your work certainly has had a dramatic effect on the drugs underworld, no surprise it's taken a lot out of you.'

They chatted non-stop through their lovely meal. David told her something of his story, then took out a memory stick.

'Have a glimpse at this, Roberta. I have five of these, one for each of my targets. They are all free for you to use as you think best.' She opened the file marked London, and leafed through the contents. It started with Alan's typed account of everything that had happened over that period then the rest of the file had typed notes and recorded CDs of the criminals' outbursts starting with vile swearing and ending with the thug's confession. Then, a signed, no doubt resentful, agreement to Alan's demands. After that followed page upon page of photographs showing in detail the hideout, and the secured victim.

'Good heavens, Alan, this is fantastic, what a brilliant story. This will make front page news for ages. Can you leave this just with me for a while until you see how I get on?'

'Yes, I will do that, Roberta. I will give you three weeks to broadcast this information widely before I hand over a full copy to the police.

'Well that's it, Roberta, I hope you make good use of the information. Together we will create hell for the swine.

'Now, one last thing. I'm staying overnight in London and hoped you might consider joining me going to the theatre and then having a late dinner at a very nice restaurant of your choice. I promise I will not say a word about drugs or crime, just a pleasant night out to enjoy your company.'

'Alan, I would love that. I was wondering how I could see you again.'

This was the first hint to him that Roberta was interested in him, not just his story. They made arrangements to meet and David walked off, using his phone to make bookings for the evening.

Roberta walked slowly back towards her office carrying the heavy briefcase. My lord, what a story this could be. The big one for her, the one that could at last catapult her into the ranks of famous writers, as was her ambition. She smiled as she also realised how much she was looking forward to seeing this man again.

She was sure that his moustache and beard were false as would be his hair piece. Without these she could imagine him being handsome. Of course, Roberta knew who he really was and had seen a photograph of him taken on a work's outing. Also, she was of course only too well aware of where he lived, about his family, and the terrible tragedy which had damaged and changed his life.

Roberta decided that this secret was hers and hers alone. There would come a time when she could discuss this all with her newspaper colleagues but not yet. No-one at her work nor her readers were to learn his true identity. Heaven help him if the underworld found out who he really was.

The pair of them enjoyed the theatre performance hugely. Then the meal later on was of top quality. They really enjoyed it and increasingly, each other's company. When her taxi arrived, she took her host into her arms and kissed him. 'Please keep in touch, Alan,' she said and he replied, 'I promise Roberta, and am known never to break them.'

David watched as she was whisked away in her taxi. Well, what a lovely evening, but that last kiss, could it be the first of many to come? Could it be that Roberta was becoming as fond of him as he felt about her?

David decided to leave a gap of a month or two before checking in with her to see if his hopes could be fulfilled.

# Chapter 15

# Mauritius

It was unbelievably still and peaceful. Apart from an occasional car engine, the only noise to disturb this glorious autumn evening in Scotland's North West Highlands was the cheep of little birds. The sun was beginning to set and a reddish-golden hue was already indicating the night to come. David lent back enjoying his view over a still Loch Ewe.

What a hectic year it had been! However, at last it was all over and he could look forward to taking up a new life again

David had decided that, no matter how much he loved his home in Poolewe, it just brought back too many painful memories. One thing he did not intend to change was his job. He found it deeply satisfying and it involved travel to some interesting places. So the sensible move for him was to look for a nice house and garden in or near Inverness.

He took another deep sip of his favourite malt whisky, Glenlivet. But what to do in the two months he had available before picking up his career again? How's about another trip to attractive Ardnamurchan? No, that, just like his home, would again remind him of how badly the past year had turned out. No, a complete break, preferably in a very stable, sunny climate and in luxurious surroundings.

As David reached to replenish his crystal tumbler, he had a brainwave. Yes, Mauritius! That had been where he had planned to take Helen away from her misery. He still had the flight and hotel reservations kindly donated to him by his company thanks to the efforts of Pam Davies.

Opening his desk, he took out his holiday file. Yes, there were the vouchers with a booking into a five-star, exclusive resort in Grande Baie. This was located in the north of the island. The reservation was for the last two weeks in

November i.e. in three weeks' time, just ideal for his plan.

David opened up his laptop, connected to the Internet, and began to research the hotel, resort and the island which was very far south in the Indian Ocean. The hotel complex looked magnificent and most importantly for him, as he was determined to improve both his fitness and his mental attitude, there was an extensive leisure and fitness complex. So he could swim, exercise, take up yoga again and then end with a very relaxing full body massage.

Now he considered whether also to offer a holiday to Margaret and Ross. They have both been through a terrible time, neither had much money, so he was sure that they would be delighted to receive a free family holiday in a beautiful part of the world. Also, the next couple of months he found from his research, were said to be the best time for stable and sun filled weather in Mauritius.

He made up his mind to extend his current booking by a week on either side i.e. go there for a month. Margaret could come for the second week and Ross the third leaving him the first week to settle in, get to know the place, and the last just for total relaxation.

Margaret and Ross were both delighted to hear his plan and the opportunity to spend a week with David in such a lovely place. The hotel was very pleased to have the additional bookings and flights proved no problem.

David's company was also very pleased to hear of his plans and to learn that he would be returning to his position as chief executive early in the next year. David had been to Mauritius once before, in fact on his honeymoon with Helen. Although, at that time he learned little about the island, being otherwise occupied!

Since then whenever the family visited a new place in a foreign country David would carry out research as he did now. He learnt that Mauritius had had a turbulent history.

Now the island seemed to place a very high priority on the tourist industry. As it was located way down south in the Indian Ocean this meant that December and January were the best two months for weather. You could expect an average daily temperature in the early to mid-twenties.

Like most of Mauritius, the lovely coral beach fronting the hotel was protected by a reef from the full range of the moods of the Indian Ocean. But the enclosed lagoon was warm and a delight for swimmers.

David flew business class to the island's airport. He wanted the extra space as he did not wish to be hassled by holiday travellers wanting to chat. After a smooth and eventless flight, they landed in the mid-afternoon. There was a friendly welcome, then a straightforward baggage check. He strolled out to the lobby. There a tall man in chauffeur's costume stood holding a placard saying Mr. David Mackay. 'Hello, sir, welcome to Mauritius, please let me take your bag, we're parked near the entrance to the terminal.'

A totally relaxed David soon found out that the young man's name was Kishan. They chatted together as David asked all about life on the island and what the crops were in the fields as they passed by. The majority of the land was developed for sugarcane. Its tall green spikes ran like a lawn all over the land. The information from his research proved correct as it took just forty minutes before Kishan pulled up to the grand entrance to the Gran Baie Hotel. A charming young lady in local costume greeted him warmly and welcomed him. After a short time filling in the obligatory paperwork a porter took his case and guided him to his suite on the top floor of the hotel overlooking the ocean. David strolled out onto his private balcony sipping from a chilled glass of very fine champagne provided by the manager with a welcome card. He sat in the comfortable sun lounger and took in the view.

Wow, wouldn't do it any justice at all. He could see the breakers from the ocean lashing the jagged reef.

He woke two hours later from his slumber feeling drowsy but refreshed. The sun was just starting to set down which combined with a gentle rumble from his stomach chimed dinnertime.

After a shave and shower, he donned his white evening suit and made his way to the cocktail bar. 'Good evening, sir,' the steward said, proffering a small tray of tempting looking mixed nuts and tropical fruits. 'What can I get you to drink?'

'I have just arrived, what would you recommend?'

'No question, sir, our speciality is the called a Baie Beach.'

'Yes please.' He said no thank you to the offer of another. David made his way to the nearest of three restaurants. Here he had a delightful meal, well accompanied by excellent French wine, then sleepily made his way back to his suite.

The next day set the pattern for what was to come. A shower, a full breakfast, a snooze by the outside pool, then a swim in the sea. After he had once again enjoyed tasting some of the local delicacies, it was time for a stroll round the extensive, landscaped grounds whilst being escorted by wandering peacocks.

Another good swim in the sea was followed by reading on the beach. Then off to the gym. Here he did not spare himself, if he was to continue eating such rich food and drink much more than his usual diet, his weight would soon balloon. Last was his visit to the Reiki masseuse. The young lady, who became his favourite was called Alika. She was tiny, probably just under 5-foot-tall, but my goodness was she strong! When she kneaded his body at times it felt as if her fingers would enter his flesh.

When Alika had completed her version of a workout, she left David alone with gently chiming, restful music. After thanking her, he returned to his room, went out to the balcony, this time with a very cold beer, and fell sound asleep before his evening's pleasures.

By the end of his first week David knew and was known by almost all of the staff. He found them naturally courteous and friendly, although his generous tips perhaps helped.

When Saturday came David got the manager's permission to travel with Kishan to collect his daughter and her family off their flight.

‘Hey look how tanned you are, Dad, you look just great,’ Margaret said after a big, welcoming hug.

She and her two men had an absolute ball. The little one loved the beach, swimming, and playing in the external huge playpark. They took two trips around the island with Kishan, seeing all the main sites of interest to tourists. The following Saturday, any sadness from waving farewell was quickly ended when his son Ross and his new partner Irene arrived. David had not met her before but soon she had him wrapped round her little finger. Again, they had an action filled brilliant week and the sun never stopped shining. Although David did feel a bit sad to say farewell to the pair, he was hugely looking forward to repeating the first week in Mauritius.

On that Monday afternoon Alika started chatting and rhythmically massaging his back then went to answer a gentle tap on the door. When his massage started again, David felt that something was very different. Her hands just did not seem the same. He turned over and looked up to see, to his amazement, a beaming Roberta saying, ‘Hello you, and can I call you David now?’

# Chapter 16

# Finale

The large DVD screen blinked out. There was a brief moment of respectful silence, then the hall erupted in loud applause. As it died down, the Chairman and the President of the Institute of Psychiatrists stood, clapping.

The Chairman said, 'Well done, Professor Tweedie. That is the deepest immersion into a troubled mind I have ever seen or listened to. Tell me, how severe is your patient's psychosis and is there any hope of some recovery?'

'No to the latter, and extremely to the former, Chairman. David has fabricated this story in such amazing, well researched detail, he even included the purchase of lever arch files for goodness' sake, plus he is obviously blessed with a very fertile imagination. Where he got the idea of the plastic eggs and the shower cabinet holding the wheelchair is simply astounding.

'Chairman and members, I have to admit feeling great sense of personal weakness and failure. David is such a fine man and has had a mainly rich and fulfilled history to date.'

The President then spoke. 'Thank you from me also, Professor Tweedie. I am sure members would agree that you are being too hard on yourself. You seem to have tried everything within your power and that was, as the Chairman said, an extremely impressive result. Tell us please, what do his family make of all this.'

'Ah, the reason I just let David start telling the story without any introduction is that I'm very sorry to tell you all that the first two chapters were strictly true.

'However, I will end by telling you the good news. David is extremely pleased with his campaign and is back at work having suffered nothing caused by his delusion. His surviving family, Margaret and Ross, have both spoken to me and are happy to go along with his story as if it all were true.'

Finale

Lightning Source UK Ltd.
Milton Keynes UK
UKHW011532160321
380450UK00001B/10